Interlude

Interlude

Lela Gilbert

WORD PUBLISHING

Dallas•London•Vancouver•Melbourne

INTERLUDE

Library of Congress Cataloging-in-Publication Data:

Gilbert, Lela.
    Interlude / Lela Gilbert.
        p. cm.
        ISBN 0–8499–3397–8 (Trade paper)
        ISBN 0–8499–3880–5 (Mass paper)
        I. Title.
    PS3557.I34223I57 1992
    813' .54—dc20   92–21871
                                                                        CIP

Printed in the United States of America

56789 OPM 987654321

1

$\mathcal{E}$ver the poet, Elisabeth Casey sat gazing at the wild October sea, occasionally scribbling lines on a legal pad. She was supposed to be listing people to invite to her upcoming wedding, writing letters to old friends, and prioritizing dozens of things to do. Instead she intermittently composed verse, daydreamed, and reminisced about all the years she'd returned faithfully to Laguna Beach to sit right here, on this very rock, in the shadow of the old stone tower.

The wind lifted her blonde hair as a drowsy, pensive mood overtook her. She was vaguely aware of the turbulent tide occasionally thundering against the rocks and sending plumes of spray sparkling across the clear California sky. And she was ever conscious of her fiancé Jon's absence, wondering how long it would be before they were together again. Most of her thoughts, however, focused on years past and on the extraordinary course of life that had brought her to this place today.

Elisabeth was a woman who understood the concept of metamorphosis—she had, in many ways, led several lives. And none of those lives had borne much resemblance to each other. The only thread of continuity was her own persona, coursing from one existence into the next, transfigured from one character into another as she moved along.

At least Shirley MacLaine had the decency to die between her past lives, she mused. *I keep changing into new people, too, but I'm stuck with the same old body.*

Betty was about to become a married woman for the second time, but not without a few fears and misgivings. Jon Surrey- Dixon, her groom-to-be, was a man who had won her heart on several counts. He enjoyed her poetry; a fact which could only mean that he knew something about who she was and liked her anyway. Jon had also proved to be spiritually in tune with her, which she found both encouraging and extraordinary. But it was an unexplainable, almost mysterious connection between them that both delighted and disturbed her.

What is it about him that makes me feel like I've known him all my life? Why do we seem so right together? Again and again her thoughts repeated the most pressing question of all: *Will it last?* The words echoed in her mind, and never seemed to be followed by a clear answer. She unconsciously touched the jeweled locket that hung at her neck, Jon's first gift to her.

Elisabeth, or Betty, as Jon preferred calling her, was ashamed of the fact that she was divorced. And the unhappiness of her previous union had left her sorely skeptical about her capacity for remaining married. Granted, she hadn't really been in love with Carlton, her first husband. But she couldn't wholeheartedly blame him for every unpleasant aspect of their failed wedlock.

Carlton had been somewhat older than she, and he was anything but a passionate lover. He had been set in his ways and detached in his involvement with her—either sarcastically critical or not there at all. Nevertheless, she was the one who walked out, leaving him with little explanation for her abrupt departure. All she really understood about it herself was that she simply could not tolerate being married to him for one more day.

Maybe I'm incapable of making a lifelong commitment. On the other hand, Jon is nothing like Carlton. Nothing at all.

She looked down at the poem she had begun writing:

> Then, spurning seas and spanning worlds,
> You smiled 'til shadows fled . . .

It somehow brought Jon's face to mind. Tears stung her eyes. How she missed him!

Elisabeth Casey and Jon Surrey-Dixon had spent less time together than either might have wished. His professional photography assignments kept him overseas much of the year, and his stopovers in California had been few and far between. Of course the couple had delighted in every moment they'd shared. But the visits always ended in tearful good-byes, the shrill whine of jet engines, and the despairing thought, *I wonder if I'll ever see him again.*

"Absence makes the heart grow fonder . . . ," Betty's father Harold Fuller had often commented with a cynical grin, ". . . for somebody else."

No wonder I'm so insecure . . . Betty couldn't help but smile at her gruff old father's peculiar brand of folk wisdom. Harold had never exactly made it his business to build up Betty's confidence. In fact, he held that self-esteem and conceit were identical. Consequently, he felt that his daughter's attractiveness and lovability should be ignored at all costs.

A wave suddenly exploded against the rocks in front of Betty and shattered her reverie. The fine mist of salty spray wet her face. Was the tide coming in or going out? Considering the sequence of the breakers and their gathering intensity, she moved to higher ground. She seated herself on the old weatherbeaten steps that led to one of the flower-skirted beach houses at the top of the cliffs.

"I've got to get something done!" she reprimanded herself aloud, frustrated by her lack of discipline. "I took the whole day off to get organized, and what do I do? I sit on the beach and daydream!"

"Excuse me?" a passing fisherman said as he stared at her curiously.

"Oh, sorry, I was talking to myself," she mumbled, shaking her head in embarrassment and immediately fixing her eyes on her legal pad. *He probably thinks I'm nuts. Well maybe he's right.*

Her unfinished poem caught her attention again, and she frowned as she searched for words. *It's not a bad poem. I wonder if Jon will like it? Maybe I'll give it to him in a wedding card . . .*

Another smile played across her face. All at once dreams of the wedding began to drift through her mind, momentarily sweeping away her various uncertainties. The little chapel would be lit with candles and fragrant with flowers. The ceremony was scheduled for the Saturday after Thanksgiving, and they would leave on a month-long trip that would find them spending Christmas in London.

She closed her eyes and tried to remember every detail of her wedding dress. It was ice-blue silk with long sleeves, a drop-waist and an ankle-length full skirt. *Blue silk. I've always wanted a blue silk dress.*

Memories carried Betty back to her early years, to yet another lifetime, to party dresses that were forever marred with bloodstains on the sleeves and necks. Skin disease had been her constant companion until her twenty-first year, and it's residual unpleasantness had affected every area of her life—most notably her personal appearance.

Two decades of itching, bleeding, and peeling skin had ended abruptly several years ago with an unexpected healing—an event that Betty could only attribute to divine intervention. Again Jon's face flickered in her mind. He thought she was beautiful, and by the time he'd met her a lot of other people thought so too. Could he have possibly loved her before, when her skin was at its worst? Probably not, she concluded.

Betty had a secret yardstick in her heart—and no one had yet measured up to it. Could someone, somewhere out there in the world have loved her, even on her ugliest, most broken-out days—a sort of Beauty-and-the-Beast tale in reverse? Perhaps some magnanimous gentleman would have overlooked her flaws and treasured her strengths. Their mutual happiness would have healed her.

Of course life had taken a different course. Her healing had happened, and a so-called Prince Charming had married her. But, unfortunately, he had turned out to be something of a toad. So here she was, ready to try again.

Oh God, help me! I get so scared sometimes.

One of the greatest sources of her present fretfulness was a simple matter of communication—she hadn't heard from Jon in more than a week. Granted, he'd been traveling in Asia where there were neither phones nor faxes—even electrical outlets were few and far between. She understood that perfectly well. She was reassured when she recalled that their relationship had survived many such separations.

But after three or four days, strange doubts always began to creep into her thoughts, subtly intruding on her peace of mind. *He doesn't miss me as much as I miss him. If he did, he wouldn't leave me. If he really missed me, he'd keep in closer touch. I know I'd keep in touch with him . . .*

These anxious thoughts made Betty more miserable than she'd ever admitted to Jon or anyone else. They made her feel guilty because she instinctively knew once she had seen Jon she had been unreasonable. They hindered her appreciation of the tender times they'd shared. And every time Jon left, these doubts haunted her, gradually and inevitably chasing away her joy.

A chill flickered along her spine. The sapphire blue sky seemed to pale. She sighed. "He says he loves me. I just have to believe it," Betty spoke out loud again, hoping that the fisherman wouldn't reappear just in time to verify her apparent insanity.

By now Betty's earlier tranquility was gone, and in its place fear was beginning to ripple and swell. She glanced at the nearly illegible poem resting on her lap and impulsively wrote one final line, almost as a silent plea.

Still burn, Love. Never die!

Betty rose to her feet and brushed the sand off her jeans. *Maybe he tried to call today while I wasn't home. Or maybe he wrote a card . . .* Impatiently, she all but ran to her car, driving at least ten miles over the speed limit all the way back to Pasadena.

Once the car was parked, she rushed to her mailbox, turned the key and yanked it open. Two bills and a catalog. Annoyed, she hurried inside and checked the answering machine. Its green light indicated one message. She played it hopefully.

"Hi, Betty! Hope you're having a great day getting your wedding organized!" Her friend and coworker Joyce Jiminez's cheery voice went on to remind her about an important conference in the morning. "Now don't forget the meeting just because you're in love."

Right. And I'm in love with a man who's forgotten I'm alive.

Frustrated, she sank into her chair and turned on the television. She restlessly flipped through all the channels, finally stopping at CNN. A grim-faced Bernard Shaw announced, ". . . Lebanon hostage Terry Anderson celebrated another birthday in captivity. His friends and family are asking people everywhere to remember the hostages . . ."

Hostages! I'm tired of hearing about the hostages!

Betty clicked off the television in irritation and glanced out the window at a smoggy horizon. She was annoyed with herself for not accomplishing anything all day. She was tired from driving too far, too fast. She was apprehensive about everything that could go wrong with her upcoming wedding.

But Betty's frustration was rooted in her silent telephone. In her empty mailbox. And in her father's oft-quoted aphorism: "Out of sight, out of mind."

If Jon were here, he'd tell me to write something . . . Jon's encouragements to put her thoughts on paper had helped Betty to understand something about herself—something she had always known in a semiconscious way. When she found the words to communicate her feelings, she was able to sort out her emotional enigmas. She sat staring at her legal pad, disregarding the paean of praise to Jon's virtues she'd penned earlier in the day.

She turned to a blank page and rather frantically began an altogether different verse. After a few moments of composition, a sly smile of satisfaction began to curve her lips.

You're going to love this one, Mr. Surrey-Dixon, she thought proudly. *And it's just exactly how I feel when you're gone!*

> I cling to a slender, shining thread,
> Suspended from God, or so someone said.
> I swing across starry heavens,
> Past chanting galaxies, howling comets.
> Embraced, then let go, on the one side of the universe,
>   Clutched at by icy fingers on the other;
> Back and forth, back and forth,
> Laughing and screaming,
> Burning and freezing,
> Soaring, soaring,
> Falling, falling.
> I cling to a slender, shining thread,
> Suspended from God, or so someone said.

Los Angeles International Airport can be a busy place on a weeknight. But Jon Surrey-Dixon's arrival at 5:00 on a Friday evening couldn't have been more ill-timed. Elisabeth had left her Pasadena office at 3:30, wildly cutting in and out of traffic, and finally arriving at the airport more than an hour later. By the time she found a parking place, it was 4:58. And by the time she found the right gate, it was 5:10. Her heart was pounding, her face was sweaty, and she longed to stop and brush her hair.

She glanced at the arrivals screen. *Naturally his flight is on time. Flights are only late when I'm early.*

Jon was wandering around, looking lost and forlorn, when she caught sight of him. His face lit up with an expression of relief. "There you are!" He dropped his carry-on bags and took her in his arms. "I'm so glad to see you—you look beautiful!"

Relaxed in his embrace, Betty stared at him in wonder, at his red hair and clear blue eyes. He was really here! All her fears vanished at the sight of his smile. Of course he loved her. How could she have doubted it for a minute?

"Are you tired?" she asked as they headed for the car, her arm through his.

"No, not too bad, actually. I slept almost all the way back. I was awfully tired when I boarded. The group hadn't slept for three nights, riding trains and buses out of the provinces. I sure missed you, Betty." His voice was soft.

"I missed you too—I kept wishing you'd call or something."

"Call?" He threw his head back and laughed. "I'm afraid there aren't many call boxes in the jungle, Betty. Believe me, if I could have called, I would have." He paused and looked at her thoughtfully. "I did bring you a present, though."

"What?" She stopped expectantly and held out her hand.

"No, no. Not now. I'll give it to you later."

"Why not now?"

"Because it's special, that's why."

"Okay, okay." Her eyes narrowed. "What is it?"

"Betty . . . no!"

She shrugged and laughed. "Well it never hurts to try. Are you here to stay 'til the wedding?"

"I'm here for the duration," he said, "unless, of course, somebody makes me an offer I can't refuse . . ."

Betty frowned at him as fiercely as possible. "That would have to be a pretty good offer!" She had arranged for him to stay in a condominium adjoining hers—a neighbor was out of town. They drove there directly.

Placing his luggage in the neighbor's condo, they sat down together in Betty's living room. Jon's arm was around Betty's shoulders, and her head rested quietly against his chest. There was a moment of silence.

"Where's my present?" she finally said, suddenly caught up in her curiosity.

"Did I say something about a present?"

"Don't toy with me, Jon!"

He reached in his pocket and pulled out a small box. "I know we decided not to do this, Betty . . ."

"Not to do what?" She opened the box and caught her breath. A spectacular diamond blinked back at her. "Jon!"

Betty was speechless. They had, indeed, decided to forego an engagement ring in lieu of an extended honeymoon. "Does this mean no honeymoon?" She looked at him suspiciously only for a moment, unable to keep her eyes off the diamond for more than a few seconds at a time.

"No, it means we're doing both—an engagement ring and a honeymoon. I couldn't help it, Betty. Try it on. See if it needs sizing."

Betty removed the birthstone ring from her left hand and ever-so-carefully slipped the diamond in its place. It was perfect. *Why would he do this with only a week to go until we're married?* she thought.

"Now maybe the other men in your life will leave you alone while I'm out of town."

"What? What other men?" Betty said as she pulled her eyes from the ring to look at Jon in disbelief.

He studied her closely. "A woman like you is bound to attract attention now and then, Betty. Don't pretend you don't."

She was stunned. *Surely he doesn't have his own insecurities and fears! Surely not!*

"I've never noticed. I never pay any attention to any-one else, and I don't think they pay attention to me, either."

He watched her face closely. It couldn't have worn a more innocent expression. Jon shook his head and chuck-led. "Well, good. Besides, it will make your wedding band look a lot more impressive. Now—are you ready to go eat? I'm starting to feel hungry. How about you?"

They talked almost ceaselessly throughout the evening. When Jon left her for a moment to call his answering ser-vice, Betty contemplated her left hand during his time away from the table. *It's almost blinding* . . . She marveled at the beauty of the blazing solitaire gem, thinking back on Jon's words. For all the world, it sounded as if he'd seriously worried about her being involved with some-one else during his absences.

It had been a while since her day-trip to Laguna and the old Victoria Beach tower. Her anxieties had ebbed and flowed continuously since that day until Jon's arrival tonight. Each had been clearly relieved at the sight of the other. Each had evidently struggled with doubt and mis-trust. Each needed the other more than either dared admit—even to themselves.

The following Monday, Betty began a leave of absence from Outreach Unlimited Ministries where she'd been working as a writer for more than a year and a half. Once Jon arrived, she knew she would be preoccupied with him and with her wedding plans.

And so she was—the two of them drove off every day to take in some part of Southern California that Jon had never seen. His New Zealand upbringing had kept him far away from the Golden State until recent years, when he had visited on assignments for various national and international magazines. Now he and Betty went to the

San Diego Zoo. To Palm Springs. To Magic Mountain. To the Queen Mary and the Spruce Goose and Catalina Island.

When they weren't making small talk about the various points of interest they were visiting, their conversations probed each other's mind and heart intensely. Something intuitively inspired them to find out all they could as quickly as possible. They were curiously driven to delve deeper and deeper, even though a lifetime of dialogue awaited them.

A week and a day before the wedding, Jon seemed distracted when he arrived at Betty's door for morning coffee. "I had a call from *Newsweek* on my answering service. They want me to do a quick job for them next week."

"Around here?" Betty asked naively.

Jon raised his eyebrows and chuckled. "Hardly. Have you ever heard of a lovely little town called Beirut?"

"What!" Betty's eyes widened. "Beirut? Isn't that where Westerners always wind up as hostages? Jon, what did you tell them? You did say no, didn't you?"

"Betty, you have no idea how much money they offered me. It's twice the normal daily rate for a job like this. And it's perfectly safe—they're giving us a Druze escort. They are militiamen from one the most powerful factions in Lebanon," he added knowledgeably.

Tears began to fill her eyes. Next week was supposed to be the most wonderful week in their lives! "You're going?" she barely whispered.

"If I go, I'll leave Sunday night and be back Thursday night."

"What do you mean 'if'? You've already made up your mind. I can tell Jon. What if something goes wrong—the wedding is Saturday!"

"They know all about that at *Newsweek*, and they said they'd get me back here no matter what. I know these guys. I've worked for them before. It's an important account Betty, and listen . . . ," he took her in his arms, seeing her begin to cry in earnest. "Shhh. Listen, now, Betty. It's only four days, Sweetheart. What's four days when we have the rest of our lives to be together?"

Wedding preparations are more work than fun, Betty scowled as she hung up the phone. *We should have eloped!* If it hadn't been for her beautiful pale blue silk dress and the lingering vision of a romantic ceremony, she might have suggested just that to Jon. Her interest in last-minute details had lagged dramatically after his unexpected call to go to Beirut. She had wanted to enjoy his company during this time, not waste it on endless minutiae.

There were flowers to be confirmed. Caterers to be instruct-ed. Guests to be directed. Travel plans to be double-checked for people like Harold Fuller, who was flying in from Oregon for the big occasion.

"It's about time you married a real man," Betty's father had rumbled, once he learned that Jon was macho enough to survive in the Southeast Asian jungle for a week. "I just hope he doesn't leave you one of these days for some cute little China doll."

"Daddy . . ." Betty started to defend Jon's fidelity, then shrugged in resignation. "It'll be good to see you."

In spite of her initial horror over Jon's impending journey, all her negative thoughts about his decision were overshadowed by floods of tenderness for him. He seemed to be responding to her the same way. They found themselves not saying a word, holding each other more closely.

His proximity to her apartment made it possible for them to spend every waking moment together. As Saturday passed from afternoon into evening, it became more and more difficult to imagine saying good night. After dinner, they lightheartedly discussed their future together. They had decided, after returning from their honeymoon, to live in Betty's condo while they looked for a larger home. Arm in arm they walked around, trying to figure out where to fit in Jon's possessions, how many items to place in storage, and what they'd need to buy.

"New towels," Jon said emphatically. "Believe me. You haven't seen my apartment in New York, Betty, and it's just as well. My towels, sheets, and half my furniture are going directly into the trash. Most of my gear isn't even worth washing, much less moving."

"Good. When we get back from England, we'll go shopping. We should have enough to buy a few towels, considering the small fortune you're making on this job of yours."

Jon looked at her sadly. He brushed his hand across her hair and kissed her forehead. "I wish I'd said no, Betty. I really do. The closer I get to leaving, the more I wish I'd said no."

"Is it too late to cancel?" she asked, barely allowing herself to hope.

"It's far too late. I'm leaving tomorrow, remember?"

To Betty's surprise, tears appeared in his eyes. She hadn't understood just how sorry he was to go. "Well, like you said, it's only for four days, Jon."

"I hope so . . ."

"What?" Betty stiffened. "What do you mean 'I hope so'? You have to come back by Saturday, Jon! You're getting married! You aren't afraid, are you?"

"To tell you the truth, I've got a sort of unsettled feeling about leaving. Maybe it's because every time I leave you I find myself worrying, thinking you'll change your mind or some such thing. I guess I shouldn't be so anxious, considering the fact that the wedding's a week from tonight."

"I have never so much as thought of leaving you, Jon. I've never even looked at another man. I really haven't."

They were in Betty's bedroom, trying to sort out which chest of drawers would stay and which would go. Suddenly, and quite unexpectedly, Jon whispered softly, "Betty, please. I want to make love to you before I leave."

From the beginning, Jon and Betty had been affectionate with each other. But for spiritual reasons of their own, they had opted to play out their courtship by the book. To keep the rules. To wait for the ring. But this unanticipated moment transcended all such determination. It caught them both off guard.

Jon enfolded her with his arms, powerfully and with great yearning. Betty looked into his eyes and brushed his face softly with her fingers.

The hours that followed were theirs alone. They slept and woke and slept again, blanketed in tenderness. No one knew—no one would ever know about this one last night together. It would remain their precious secret forever.

Sunday morning they bypassed church and went out to breakfast. A new serenity shrouded the day with warmth, and an incomparable sense of belonging. However, as the hours passed, Jon's departure grew closer. Around 2:30 Betty sadly watched as he packed his camera gear, hung his clothes in his flight bag, and zipped his carry-on shut.

"Are you sure you can't call somebody and say you're desperately ill?"

"I am feeling a little sick, to tell you the truth. It makes me sick to leave you, Sweetheart. I was a fool to take this assignment. Greedy and foolish."

"Well, you had to pay for my diamond, remember?"

"Maybe I'll bring you another one—for the other hand." He kissed her right hand wistfully and then checked his watch. "I guess we'd better head out for the airport."

The lengthy ride to the airport was filled with nervous conversation, both Betty and Jon trying to be relaxed and casual for the other's benefit. When they came to the terminal, they found that the British Airways flight to London was on time. Jon checked his bags, watched while the airline representative examined his passport, and started for the gate.

"Now tell me again—what's happening once you get to London?"

"Beirut airport is open at the moment, so I'm meeting a writer in London, catching a Middle East Airlines flight, and arriving in Beirut Monday night their time. Beirut time is ten or eleven hours ahead of California. We're shooting all day Tuesday and part of Wednesday. I fly out on MEA Wednesday afternoon, catch a return flight home and will be back Thursday night around 11:00 P.M."

"Those sound like pretty close connections."

"It's all confirmed—all the way through. There's no problem, Betty. Just pray for me, and I'll pray that you get everything done on this end."

Impulsively, Jon pulled her toward him and held her tightly against his chest. "Lord, take care of my precious Betty. You know she's my wife now, and I'm her husband, 'til death do us part. I pray that You'll keep her safe until I get back. Make me a good husband to her, Lord— the best she could ever have. And while I'm gone, please bless her and keep her and make Your face shine upon her. In Jesus' name, Amen."

"Amen . . ." Betty whispered, bracing herself for his actual departure. *No tears*, she commanded her eyes sternly. "Good-bye, Jon. I'll see you in four days."

"Just four days!" he said brightly, kissing her once more and heading for the big 747. He turned once more, blew her another kiss, and he was gone.

Betty drove back to Pasadena, unable to focus her thoughts on anything but Jon and the brief time that they had enjoyed together since her last solo trip to the airport. Would it always be like this? Would home be only a stopover between jobs? Would he always return? Their times together had been the most wonderful times of her life. Would it always be like that? The sweetness of their intimacy filled Betty with a fleeting sense of joy as she tearfully steered her car across the light-spangled city.

Clearly, the love she and Jon shared was a given. It had been there all along, even amidst their worst doubts. Nevertheless, one contrary thought could be heard whispering in the farthest reaches of her mind. It was completely incompatible with her mood, yes. But a faint but familiar question still remained unanswered: *Will it last?*

2

The first two days after Jon's departure were hectic, and in one sense Betty was glad he was gone. All their frenetic sightseeing had kept her from following up on some very necessary wedding preparations. For the most part she was able to put him out of her mind while she phoned, ran errands, and wrote a rather sobering succession of checks. The sight of the twinkling diamond on her left hand invariably reminded her of him, and she couldn't help but smile.

Tuesday night she collapsed in bed, exhausted. *Two days more and he'll be home*, she reminded herself as she drifted off to sleep. *I can't wait to see him.* Halfway through the night the telephone awoke her. She fumbled to turn on a light. *It must be Jon,* she reasoned.

"Hello?" Her voice was thick with sleep.

"Ma'am, this is George O'Ryan with the State Department in Washington, D.C. Is this Mrs. Jon Surrey-Dixon?" The crisp, businesslike voice on the other end of the line brought her closer to wakefulness.

"No, this is Elisabeth Casey, Jon's fiancée."

"Elisabeth Casey. So you are you the fiancée, not the wife of Jon Surrey-Dixon, a freelance photographer who recently traveled to Lebanon?"

"Yes, I'm Jon's fiancée." She drew a quick breath. "Is he all right?"

"Ms. Casey, I'm afraid I have some unpleasant news for you. We have a confirmed report out of Beirut that your fiancé was abducted by Islamic terrorists on his way into the city from the airport. Fortunately his colleagues were left behind—he was the only one taken."

Silence. What could she possibly say?

"Ms. Casey, are you still on the line?"

"Yes, I'm here. What do I do? Who should I talk to?"

"Although it is not our policy to tell hostage family members what to do, I would strongly advise you not to talk to the media at this time. We hope to have this matter resolved quickly. I understand that your fiancé is a naturalized American—is that true?"

"No, he's not an American citizen. He has a green card, but he carries a New Zealand passport."

"I see. I'll double-check that. Is there anything I can help you with, then?"

"Well, yes. What are you doing about Jon? Are you trying to get him out? We're getting married on Saturday."

Why did her words about the wedding sound so shallow and foolish?

There was a brief pause. O'Ryan seemed to be processing unexpected information. "I see. Well, I'm sure you're aware that it is official U. S. policy not to negotiate with terrorists. We are doing all we can on behalf of all the hostages in Lebanon, and we are optimistic that this crisis will come to a swift conclusion." The man sounded like he was reading from a script, and his platitudes couldn't have been less comforting.

By now Betty was wide awake. "Could you give me your name again, please? And your phone number?" She wrote down the information, and at his request gave him her address.

His answers had been so unsatisfactory that she repeated her question a third time. "Isn't there anything I can do?"

"Nothing, ma'am. The less you do, the better. The more attention you draw to the kidnapping, the more valuable your fiancé becomes to his abductors. Please contact me if you have any further questions."

"Well, I'm going to have to tell my friends and family."

"I'm sure they'll hear about it through the usual sources. The news media are quick to report these things," O'Ryan replied rather haughtily.

"Are you sure I can't do something? Talk to someone? Jon's not even an American citizen—maybe the people that took him think he is. Maybe they should be told that he's from . . ."

"Ms. Casey, as I said before, the less you do the better. We're professionals. Leave it with us."

The conversation, such as it was, seemed to be over. "Thank you for calling," Betty could hardly believe she was expressing gratitude for such devastating news.

"Yes, ma'am. We'll be in touch."

She rested the phone in its cradle. Her diamond sparkled in the dim light. She stared at it blindly.

They'll get him out soon, she tried to reassure herself. *He just didn't want to get my hopes up.* But despite her attempts at optimism, a heavy darkness seemed to be settling across her mind. Then an idea flashed. *CNN! Maybe they've got something on CNN!*

She turned on the television just in time to see Jon's picture flicker morbidly on the screen. The quality of the black-and-white photograph was terrible, but she could clearly see that it was Jon. One eye was swollen shut. His upper lip appeared distorted. His eyes looked blank, as if he were dazed.

Nausea almost overwhelmed her. She began to shiver violently, her teeth chattering wildly. She tried to concentrate on the words coming out of the television.

"... Jon Surrey-Dixon, the latest victim of Islamic terrorist kidnappings, is thirty-five years old. Although he is a native New Zealander, he carries an American green card. ..."

I wonder why CNN knew that and the state department didn't? Despite Betty's shock, she couldn't help but notice the discrepancy in information.

"... His fiancée Elisabeth Casey is a writer, living in Pasadena, California. Surrey-Dixon and Casey were to have exchanged vows Saturday, a wedding that will clearly be postponed indefinitely. ..."

They got that right, too.

"... We hope to have some comment from Elisabeth Casey in the next hour. ..."

Postponed indefinitely. Comment from Elisabeth Casey. How do they know all this? She felt watched. Frantic, she clicked off the television and opened the blinds, checking for intruders outside. The street was empty.

What do I say to them if they come here? She was terrified. Did they have her phone number? The United States of America Department of State had "strongly advised" her not to talk to the media. Would she be breaking some kind of law if she did? Would she endanger Jon's life if she said anything at all?

Wild surges of fear ebbed and flowed inside her. The

image of Jon's bruised face was indelibly imprinted on her mind. "God! Help me! What do I do?"

The phone rang again. This time it was CNN. How had they located her so quickly? She never thought to ask. "Ms. Casey . . . Sorry to bother you at such a terrible time. Tell me, how do you feel? What was your reaction to the news?"

Now the tears began. "I don't know what to say . . . I don't know what to say. Just pray for Jon, that's all I can say . . ."

The female journalist who called sounded far more compassionate than O'Ryan. "I'm so sorry about this tragedy, Ms. Casey," she said. "We've been covering this hostage situation for years, and it just breaks my heart. If I can ever do anything to help you, please give me a call."

The woman gave Betty both a work and a home number. It seemed like a generous gesture at the moment.

In less than an hour's time, Betty's plaintive words, "I don't know what to say. I don't know what to say . . ." were broadcast around the globe. Her voice was heard in dozens of countries. In bars and palaces. In airports and hotel lobbies. Her personal loss had instantly become a matter of common knowledge. Her private tears were public domain. Betty's love story was no longer her own.

The wedding was canceled. Jon Surrey-Dixon was a hostage. The world was watching.

Betty sat in her chair from 4:30 until 6:00 A.M. unable to sleep, almost paralyzed with fear. There were no more calls until Jim Richards at Outreach Ministries International telephoned at 6:10.

"Betty, I just heard the news about Jon. It's on all the networks. Are you all right?"

"No . . ."

"Are you getting bombarded by the press?"

"No, at least not yet."

"Look, I'm going to pick up Joyce and we're coming over there. I think you need a couple of friends right now. Is that okay with you?"

"Thanks, Jim. Yeah. Go ahead and come." Her voice had no inflection.

Betty dislodged herself from the chair and made her way to the shower. She went through the motions of dressing herself, drying her hair, and putting on her makeup. *Waterproof mascara,* she instructed herself. *You've got enough black circles under your eyes already, and you know you're going to cry all day.*

Oddly enough, however, she hadn't shed that many tears. Her feelings were muffled and dulled, except for an ache of acute weariness.

Not a half-hour after his call, Jim pushed Joyce Jiminez' wheelchair into Betty's living room. Joyce was a rheumatoid arthritis sufferer, who single-handedly managed Jim's international humanitarian organization in spite of her physical limitations. She was also a remarkably spiritual woman.

"Betty . . ." Joyce and Betty were close, dear friends. The minute Joyce's arms found their way around Betty's neck, the tears began. Joyce was weeping too.

"I hate to tell you this, Betty," Jim interrupted. "But there are several network vans outside and a whole bunch of reporters. I think you'd better go out there and say something. You don't want to get on their bad side."

"But Jim, when the man from the State Department called, he strongly advised me not to talk to the media."

"That's pretty unrealistic, isn't it?"

Betty looked at Jim in surprise. It had never occurred to her to question orders from Washington, D.C.

"Well it really is pretty difficult, since they call and show up uninvited. I guess I ought to be able to say something. They're just doing their job."

"Why don't you just say that you love Jon, you're hoping to see him soon, and then ask everyone to remember him in prayer?" Joyce recommended.

Betty considered Joyce's suggestion uncertainly. Joyce's ideas always seemed so simple, almost too obvious. "I just don't want to make a mistake."

"Why would that be a mistake? Even the kidnappers are supposed to be religious. How could anyone complain about you asking people to pray for Jon?"

"What do you think, Jim?"

"You know Joyce is always right." Jim and Joyce had worked together for years, and behind his friendly banter was a sincere respect for the tiny Hispanic woman who had given so much of herself to their ministry.

"Betty," Joyce's crippled hand reached for her friend's, "let's pray before you go out there."

"You pray, Joyce. Right at the moment I feel like God's locked up in a cell with Jon. You'd better do the praying."

The three of them held hands, and Joyce began, "Lord, we don't understand what You're doing in this. We don't know why You've allowed this to happen to Jon and to Betty. But we love You and trust You. Please, Lord, give Betty wisdom and strength as she speaks to those reporters out there. Let her represent You to them. And somehow, Heavenly Father, help her feel Your presence and give her peace. Give us all peace . . ."

The phone rang, and just as Betty answered it the doorbell chimed. Jim went to the door. "Here we go . . ." he murmured to himself.

"We'll be having a press conference in fifteen minutes,"

Jim told the journalists outside. "It's a sunny day, so why don't you set up your cameras here," he motioned toward Betty's small patio, "and that way she won't have a houseful of people she doesn't know . . ."

Betty had never thought about holding a "press conference." And it certainly had never occurred to Betty that Jim might know how to manage one. Over the years he had been involved in several international incidents that had been covered by the world press. Whatever he had learned along the way was welcome information to Betty, who was totally ignorant in such matters.

"Who was on the phone?"

"A reporter from the Associated Press."

"You're going to have to change the message on your answering machine. Don't answer the phone any more. Just screen your calls, talk to whoever you want and forget the rest."

Betty nodded mutely. *What if Jon calls and I don't answer?* She knew he couldn't call, but what if somehow, some way he tried and couldn't get through? Sorrow weighed heavily against her chest. Suddenly she missed him more.

"I'm going out there now, Jim. Why don't you come with me?"

"Do you know what you're going to say? Do you need to write something down?"

"No, I'm fine, Jim."

She was startled at the sight of several dozen men and woman standing on her patio. Videocam lights bathed her in an unearthly glow. Motor drives whirred. Shutters clicked.

"Ladies and gentlemen," Jim said, "this is Elisabeth Casey, Jon Surrey-Dixon's fiancée. As I'm sure you can imagine, she is facing a staggering tragedy and has only been aware of Jon's kidnapping for about three hours.

She will make a brief statement, and she may answer a few questions."

Jim's strong, calm voice brought a sense of order to the impromptu conference. He nodded to Betty, indicating that she should go ahead.

"I'm Elisabeth Casey." She looked into eyes intently focused on her face. Nervousness made her hands tremble and her voice waver.

"At four-thirty this morning I received a call from the State Department advising me that my fiancé, Jon Surrey-Dixon, had been kidnapped in Beirut. We were to be married Saturday, and as you can imagine, I'm devastated by this news. I don't know anything about Lebanon, or the hostages, or anything else. I just want to ask people to pray for Jon and for the others too. I think there are six or seven other hostages? That's all I have to say. Please pray for us all."

A flurry of questions followed.

"Where are his parents?"

"Jon's parents are dead."

"Are there other relatives?"

"He's never . . . not that I know of, at least not here."

"What is the U.S. government doing to get him out?"

"Are you sure he's alive?"

"What about the rest of his family?"

The reporters were all shouting at the same time. Muddled by all the confusion and unsure about how much she should say, Betty thanked them all, excused herself quickly, and fled back inside her home. Joyce was watching the television. "You were live on all three networks, Betty. You did a great job."

The phone rang and continued to ring incessantly all day. Nearly every major newspaper in the country called, along with several wire services and television news programs. Betty desperately tried to limit her comments to as few as possible, and again and again she found herself saying more than she wanted.

Why on earth would journalists be asking for her opinion about U.S. foreign policy? Or Middle East politics? Or Israeli human rights violations? The flurry of inquiries frightened and exhausted her. And, in the midst of it all, the horrifying picture of Jon's bruised and battered face continued to play in her memory over and over again.

"Somehow, Joyce, I've got to find time to cancel the wedding." She shook her head sadly. "I don't even know where to begin . . ."

Joyce turned to Jim, "What if I stay here with Betty today? The office can survive without me. I'll help her get things or-ganized. Maybe you'd like to bring us some lunch around noon. I don't think Betty's going to feel much like going out, and neither am I."

Jim grinned. "Of course I'll bring lunch. I've been chief gopher for OMI long enough to know my place."

Jim left and the calls gradually diminished. Betty wanted to keep tuned into CNN, in case there might be some change in Jon's situation. Somehow she kept dragging her feet about canceling the wedding. *Maybe they'll decide to let him go and he'll be back by Saturday!* It was an absurd hope, but she clung to it fiercely.

Joyce watched her friend carefully throughout the day. Perhaps her own illness had made her especially sensitive to other people's pain. Or maybe she was just intuitive. But she quietly said, "Betty, I think you should turn off the television, turn the phone down so it doesn't ring, and rest for a while."

"What if someone calls about Jon? What if Jon calls?" Betty was becoming obsessed with the idea that he might suddenly emerge from his ordeal.

"Okay, I understand. Look, I'll answer the phone, and I'll wake you if there's any word about Jon. But you have got to get some rest. You're on the edge, Betty. Where is your wedding file? I'll make some calls for you. I have a feeling everyone's heard about Jon by now."

The phone rang again. This time it was Harold, Betty's father.

"I just saw you on TV." He sounded uncharacteristically gentle. "Betty, I'm sorry about this hostage mess Jon's gotten himself into. I really am. I'm going to call some of my old Marine buddies and see if they know anything. A couple of guys are still on active duty."

"That's a good idea, Daddy. The man at the State Department sure didn't have much to tell me."

"That's because he's a paper pusher. He doesn't know anything himself. Haven't you ever heard about bureaucrats?"

In his own way, Harold had softened toward Betty since his wife Lucilla's death. And now, oddly enough, his words had a quieting effect upon his daughter. After his call, she went to her room and drifted off to sleep, soon dreaming of the heartwarming times she and Jon had shared.

An hour later she woke suddenly, a monstrous thought overshadowed her mind. Was God judging her and Jon for their intimate liaison just days before? Had her moral lapse somehow led to Jon's abduction? Were they paying the piper for their tender dance?

"Oh God, I'm sorry," she murmured as feelings of guilt engulfed her. "Please—don't punish him. It was my fault. I should have said no!"

In the three days that followed Jon's kidnapping, Betty appeared on ABC, NBC, and CBS national news. She was interviewed by Larry King, Ted Koppel, and the "Good

Morning, America" team. Makeup was blotted on her
face, wiped off, and sponged on again as she went from
interview to interview.

Her sudden loss seemed to catch the imagination of
people all over the country. From Wednesday through
Saturday her phone rang continuously, photographers
came and went, and friends stayed by Betty's side. The
tale of the tragically canceled wedding was the coast-to-
coast human-interest story of the week. She hardly had
time to mourn, consider her personal guilt, or even think
about Jon himself. Ceaseless distractions anesthetized
her, but when she slept the image of Jon's injured face
awakened her several times a night.

Then, without warning, the focus of the news media
shifted to other world crises. To the stock market. To
Russia. To Saddam Hussein. Betty's phone fell silent. Her
friends had to go back to work. "I'll be fine," she assured
them with a smile.

But she was not.

She awakened Monday morning with no place to go
and nothing to do. Her leave of absence was still in effect
at OMI, and she couldn't have concentrated on writing
even if she'd gone back to work. At 10:00 A.M., after scour-
ing every page of the *L.A. Times* for the vaguest reference
to Jon, she went back to bed, pulled the covers over her
head and tried to sleep.

She rolled and tossed for an hour. The phone rang.
Hope stirred inside her, and she leaped to her feet to
answer it. "Hello?"

"This is the *Los Angeles Times*."

"Yes?" Again, a surge of hope.

"Would you be interested in a three-month sub-
scription . . ."

She angrily slammed the receiver back down.

I've got to get dressed and do something with myself. She took a shower, wrapped herself in a towel and went to the closet to find something to wear. As she moved the sliding door, there was her beautiful pale blue silk wedding dress, covered with plastic, awaiting the ceremony that had never come. She reached for it, about to hang it in some out-of-sight corner. Then hope teased her. *Leave it there . . . maybe he'll be back this week.*

She looked at the diamond on her hand. At the dress in the closet. At the picture of Jon on her bureau. An overwhelming sense of powerlessness gripped her. Trying to shake it off, she reached for a pair of jeans and an old shirt.

A sense of impotence persisted. Jon had been there with her—right there in that room—just a week before. And surely he was alive somewhere, right now, at this moment, today. He loved her. She loved him. But there was nothing in the world she could do to reach him. No letter could be delivered. No phone call could be connected. No telex. No fax. Nothing.

Angry and downhearted, she pulled on her jeans and buttoned her shirt.

When she thought about Jon, she realized that he was far more helpless than she. From what she'd been told by the journalists who had covered the hostage situation for years, Jon Surrey-Dixon was chained to a wall in some filthy basement in West Beirut. He was blindfolded and stripped to his underwear. He was allowed one trip to the bathroom every day. He was fed stale pita bread, cheese, and olive oil. He wouldn't see the sun, moon or stars until the day of his release. He wouldn't smell flowers, feel the wind, or hear the rain.

Betty crumpled to the floor. "Oh God!" she cried out, "Are You there? I feel like You've left me here all alone. I can't bear it, Lord. Haven't I been through enough in my life without this? Please—do something quickly about Jon. You can do anything. Can't You just set him free? And what about me? Can I do anything? Lord, please . . ."

A thought interrupted her frantic prayer. *Be still and know that I am God.* It was a memory verse from some long-ago Sunday school lesson, and seemed incongruous in the midst of all her pain.

"God, what are You going to do about Jon?" Her voice was demanding.

She grabbed a hairbrush and tried to pull it through her wet hair. Clicking on the television, she watched CNN just long enough to see that "Moneyline" was on. She began to flip through the other channels. When she came to channel 40, she paused.

Some pompadoured preacher she didn't recognize was smiling at her, saying something incomprehensible. She turned up the volume. He had an exceptionally strong Southern accent. *Good grief, Christian programming can be so predictable.*

"'Be still and know that I am God.' This is God's message to you today, dear friend . . ."

In spite of her sardonic attitude, Betty couldn't help but listen.

"'Be still.' That means quiet your mind, Sister, and silence your frantic thoughts. 'Know' is more than believing, Brother. It's accepting something as fact. And what does 'I am God' mean? It means that Somebody bigger than you and I has your life in His capable hands. 'Be *still* and *know* that *I am God*' means 'relax, let go, and let God take care of everything.'"

Betty stared at the television preacher. His well-rehearsed smile annoyed her almost as much as his Southern drawl. But she couldn't find fault with his words.

She turned off the television, got up, and started walking aimlessly around the house.

Be still.
Know.
I am God.

The message was clearly intended for her. An answer to her demand for help? What was she supposed to do with it?

I won't do a thing today, she decided after a few minutes. *I'll relax as much as possible. If God wants me to be still, I'll be still. Besides*, she confided in the remarkably haggard face that stared back at her from the bathroom mirror, *I can use the rest.*

The doorbell rang Monday afternoon and awakened Betty from a deep sleep. The postman was on the porch holding a container filled with mail. "I've got so much stuff for you, I can't get it all in your mailbox," he said. "By the way, I saw on TV what happened to your boyfriend. I hope they get him out soon!"

"Thanks. So do I. Boy, that is a lot of mail, isn't it? Why don't you dump it on the table?"

Once he was gone, she began sorting through the cards and letters, pulling out those with handwriting she recognized and opening them first. She was touched by the outpouring of good wishes, most of which were from strangers who had simply addressed them to, "Elisabeth Casey, Pasadena, California." The postal service had been kind enough to find her.

She heard from several old friends. Woody and Sharon, schoolmates on sabbatical from their mission in Africa. Irina Mandaley, her mentor from years before. Leah, her fellow fashion model. Even her ex-husband Carlton had sent a thinking-of-you card, signed "Best Regards, Carlton Casey." *Well, at least he took the time to write.* She felt somewhat gratified by his courtesy.

There was a note from a woman in Seattle who said she prayed for the hostages every day. A letter from a New York Jesuit priest who expressed his concern as well as his rather curious political insight.

I wonder if I'm supposed to answer all these letters? The thought of going out and buying thank you cards and stamps, and responding to each communiqué made her feel utterly weak.

An elegantly embossed blue envelope caught her eye. She opened it to find a note from a classmate from Los Angeles Bible College. The note said, "You may find it surprising to learn that I am married to Kenneth Townsend, a priest in the Episcopal church. Our parish in Orange Hills is very involved in addressing social concerns and humanitarian causes.

"When Ken and I saw you on television, we talked about what we could do to help. We decided to invite you to a small dinner party with some key people from our church. Perhaps we could pray with you about providing support for you during this crisis.

"Please call me and we'll make the arrangements. The Lord be with you, Betty.

"In Him, Erica West Townsend."

Betty had always liked Erica in spite of the fact that she had been a straight A student who always looked wonderful. Betty could recall running into her in the girls' dorm and thinking that Erica even looked perfect in her jammies. In those days Betty had been anything but a fashion plate, and could not imagine having a neat-as-a-pin appearance, if her life had depended upon it.

It occurred to her that Erica hadn't seen her since her skin disease had vanished. Erica would also realize that Betty was divorced—she'd known her as Betty Fuller, and the newspapers and television stories were talking about Elisabeth Casey. Betty always felt uncomfortable seeing old friends who hadn't heard the bad news about her first marriage—especially now that her postponed second wedding was an international story.

Maybe Episcopalians aren't as concerned about divorce as the Baptists I grew up with. They're too busy ordaining homosexual priests to care about such minor details. Betty smirked at her own brand of judgmentalism while dialing Erica's number.

"Hello, Erica? This is Betty Fuller—or Elisabeth Casey if you're watching television."

"Betty, how are you? I've been so worried about you! Are you all right?"

"Oh, I don't think I'm really all right at all. But I appreciate your concern, Erica. It was so nice of you to think of me."

"How would you feel about coming to a dinner party?"

"I'd be honored, of course. Are you sure you want to go to that much trouble?"

"It's not trouble at all! It's a pleasure . . ."

The dinner was planned for the following Friday night. Betty hung up feeling both curious and apprehensive. She remembered all too well her mother Lucilla's attitude toward those of religious denominations other than her own. Generally speaking, Lucilla felt they had all missed the narrow way into heaven by several thousand light-years.

Oh, what difference does it make? They want to pray for me and support me—there's nothing wrong with that, is there? Besides, Jon's Catholic, and that's even worse than being Episcopalian, at least by Mother's standards.

Friday night found Betty driving down the 57 Freeway toward Orange Hills. She followed Erica's precise directions and parked in front of a large contemporary house with a broad lawn. She was just a few minutes late. When the door opened, she found herself in the company of four couples and three single women.

Erica embraced her affectionately. "Betty, you look wonderful! Your face . . . what is it that's so different? You used to have some sort of rash, didn't you?"

"Yes, to put it mildly. But that's another story for another day, Erica."

"Well, you look absolutely wonderful," Erica repeated and introduced her to the others, who greeted her warmly. She was led into a well-appointed living room, given a glass of chilled white wine, and surrounded by the others. There was no question about who was to be the center of attention that evening. Betty, her plight, and her needs were all anyone wanted to discuss.

After a buffet dinner, while the guests were still seated around the huge glass-top table, Ken Townsend said, "Betty, before we go to the other room, I'd like for us all to join hands and pray for you. Would you be comfortable with that?"

"Of course I would. I need your prayers very much." She looked at the kind faces of the people who sat around the table. They didn't appear to be an overly affluent looking group, but they had obviously dressed up for the evening—for *her* evening.

"You know, it's been hard for me to pray since Jon was kidnapped . . ." her voice broke unexpectedly. "I feel like there's something wrong between God and me. Maybe He's not there or He's angry. I don't know . . ."

Again the mental image of her final, intimate night with Jon came to her mind, and with it came the usual ambivalence. She sighed and looked at the table.

"Betty, I can promise you that God isn't angry, and

He's not only *with* you, He's *in* you." Ken's voice was gentle and kind.

"Well, I've done some things I'm not proud of . . ."

"Haven't we all?" Everyone at the table laughed. Betty looked around at them gratefully.

A woman spoke softly, "I have a sense that you're blaming yourself somehow for Jon's kidnapping, Betty. I don't know you, but I feel in my spirit that you should reject any guilt you're feeling and believe that God has a higher purpose in this situation than anything you can possibly understand. 'My ways are above your ways,' the Lord says. You mustn't feel responsible, dear."

In a way she barely understood, Betty felt a release in her spirit. No, God wasn't punishing her for making love to Jon. *If God handled premarital sex that way, Lebanon wouldn't have room for all the hostages!* She almost laughed out loud at the thought.

"Thank you," she said to the woman, whose name she couldn't even recall. "I think, at least I hope, that you spoke for the Lord. I needed to hear that."

Ken nodded. "Let's join hands and pray together." One by one, each of those people, strangers to her until that occasion, took Betty's heavy burden upon himself. Each one prayed about some aspect of her separation from Jon. Not one man prayed for himself; not one woman expressed concern for her own needs. They gave of themselves wholeheartedly in prayer, and when they were finished they offered their time, their money, their homes—anything they could think of that might alleviate Betty's suffering. She could hardly believe her ears.

Just before the evening ended, a distinguished looking gentleman spoke to his wife quietly and the two took Betty aside. "I work for a news syndicate with a large bureau in Washington, D.C. I've seen something on the wire about a hostage family gathering in Washington in early January. Once I've confirmed the fact that it's really happening, Doris and I would like to pay your way there and also take care of your hotel accommodations. From what I understand, it's quite encouraging for the various hostage family members and friends to meet together now and then, along with some of the ex-hostages. Would you like to go?"

Betty looked at him in amazement. "I . . . I've never been to Washington, D.C."

"Well, I'll see that someone meets your plane and gets you to your hotel. Don't worry about that. And we'll try to make some preparations for you to meet people like Peggy Say and some of the other family members."

"Who's Peggy Say?"

"She's Terry Anderson's sister, and she's been a spokesperson for the families since 1985."

After a moment, Betty said, "Your offer is so generous that it's hard for me to accept it. But yes, I think I should go. At least I won't be sitting at home waiting for the phone to ring."

"Betty," the man spoke kindly, while his wife wrote down her phone number and address, "you may be waiting for the phone to ring for a long time. Some people have been waiting for more than half a decade. But you're not waiting alone. From now on every person here will be waiting with you."

Betty looked around the room. The dinner guests were putting on their coats and saying their last good-byes. "You know, I feel like I've known you for years," she said to Erica, Ken, and all the others.

Erica smiled, "Well, there's a Psalm that says 'God sets the solitary in families.' We'll be your family if you'll let us."

Christmas lights sparkled along the streets and freeways, and the night wind blew cold and crisp. As she made her way home across the Orange County suburbs, Betty's eyes swam with tears from time to time. For the moment, it was not sadness that flooded them. Something else was stirring inside her—a strange, inexpressible emotion. There were no words to explain it, no theology to define it. But unexpectedly, in the presence of those benevolent Episcopalian people, she had glimpsed the tender heart of God.

Suddenly some long-forgotten lyrics to a well-loved hymn came to her like a voice from heaven, affirming the embrace of the Father.

> Every day the Lord Himself is near me
> With a special mercy for each hour;
> All my cares He fain would bear, and cheer me,
> He whose name is Counselor and Power.
> The protection of His child and treasure
> Is a charge that on Himself He laid;
> 'As thy days, thy strngth shall be in measure,'
> This the pledge to me He made.

3

_____

The envelope was from the Golden Bay Hotel in Larnaca, Cyprus. Betty ripped it open with shaky fingers.

Dear Betty,

I'm the writer who was assigned to the Beirut story with your fiancé Jon, and I was with him when he was kidnapped. I found your address and phone number in his diary and thought I should write you. He and I were traveling together and of course he had told me that you and he were to be married on the following Saturday. His luggage and camera equipment were in our car, so I kept it. I'll be shipping it to you when I get back to the States—it's very heavy and too expensive to ship from here.

Although I am still on the road covering a couple of other aspects of the Beirut story, I will be back in the U.S. in early January. I will try to telephone you then and tell you in detail about the kidnapping.

Don't give up on that wedding—Jon cares for you very much. Please accept my sincere sympathy about the tragedy.

All the best,
Vince Angelo

Betty's hands were shaking even more by the time she finished reading the letter. For the first time she was confronted with a violent scene that had actually happened—an occurrence she hadn't allowed herself to think about before. Someone had witnessed the abduction. He had seen firsthand the abuse Jon had suffered. Heard his words. Seen his fear. Vince Angelo had escaped, free and unharmed. Jon Surrey-Dixon hadn't.

I don't know whether I want to meet this guy or not. I wonder if he knows anything that could help Jon? Surely the Army or the Navy or somebody has talked to him by now. I wonder who's in charge of this case, anyway? I sure hope it isn't George O'Ryan at the State Department. If he's running the show, I'll never see Jon again!

The letter immobilized Betty for several hours. She reverted to her old, helpless pattern of sitting in her chair, turning on the television, turning it off again, trying to read, and finally staring straight ahead. This time, after a catatonic hour or two, she picked up the phone and dialed her father's phone number.

"Hi, Daddy, it's me."

"How are you doing?"

"Oh, fine, I guess."

"Any news about your boyfriend?"

"Not really. That's why I called. Listen, did you ever get a hold of any of your old Marine buddies like you said you would?"

"Yeah, in fact I called up Red Jeffrey yesterday. He's stationed up Seattle way, and he knows an officer there who was over in Beirut when the Marine barracks got blown up back in '83. He's gonna talk to the guy and see what he knows."

"Daddy, who's in charge of getting the hostages out? That's what I want to know."

Harold paused. "You mean which branch of government?"

"I mean what person is responsible. Who's at the top?"

"Well, the president, I guess, at least now that Ollie North's gone. People complained about Ollie, you know, but he's a no-nonsense Marine, and he got more hostages out than anybody ever has, before or since."

"Right. Semper Fi." Betty closed her eyes, awaiting a further tribute to the U.S. Marine Corps from her father. Instead he said, "What are you doing for Christmas?"

"I can't even think about Christmas."

"Well you'd better think about it. It's less than three weeks away. Why don't you come up here?"

"I'm afraid to leave the phone, Daddy. What if Jon gets out?"

"So you're going to sit there alone all day? Why don't you get one of those machines . . . ?"

"You mean an answering machine? I've got one."

"Well, then, use it. Come on up here and I'll see if Red can come by and meet you. I think he's going to be around here during the holidays. You can talk to him about who's heading up the hostage detail."

Betty tried to fight off a vague fear that she shouldn't leave the house—staying home had become almost a fixation. "I'll think about it, Daddy. And if you talk to Red again, tell him I'd appreciate anything he can find out."

She hung up the phone trying to remember everything she'd ever heard about the Lebanese hostages. She faintly recalled the bombing of the French and American barracks in 1983. Since that time an odd assortment of hapless victims' faces had paraded across television screens. She recalled seeing Terry Anderson, Anglican envoy Terry Waite, and a couple of others whose names eluded her.

But what she wanted to know the most she understood the least—who in the American government had the job of getting the captives out?

Preparing to go to Oregon for Christmas gave Betty something to do, but she had no enthusiasm for the trip. She picked up the phone several times to cancel, but she couldn't bring herself to tell Harold, "Sorry, I just can't make it."

She was trying to establish her relationship with her father on more solid ground. Closeness with him had evaded her all her life, and it seemed that this present crisis had somehow given them common cause. And besides that, she couldn't help but wonder what his Marine friend Red would have to say.

Betty suspected that Red Jeffrey was a right-wing know-it-all, but she still wanted to talk to him. She certainly wasn't about to call the State Department for information.

She hadn't yet found the courage to contact other hostage families either, although she had their phone numbers. Her plight seemed so insignificant compared to theirs. Some of them had been waiting for five or six years for a release and couldn't even be sure their loved ones were still alive. Why on earth would they want to hear from her?

Thus far, her only background source on the subject had been the myriad journalists who contacted her when

Jon was first abducted. They had given her bits and pieces of the story, and what she learned made no sense.

For example, what distinguished the little groups that took credit for kidnapping the various hostages? The Islamic Jihad. The Islamic Holy War for the Liberation of Palestine. The Revolutionary Justice Organization. Jon's kidnappers had called themselves the Islamic Revolutionary Organization. Supposedly he was their first victim. No statement had been issued regarding demands, ransom or anything else. Who were the kidnappers? What did they want? Why did they take Jon?

The day before she left for Oregon, a Christmas card arrived from Kentucky. Inside it was a note,

> Dear Elisabeth,
>
> I just wanted you to know that you are in my thoughts and prayers this holiday season. I know how painful this time of year can be for you, and I hope you'll keep yourself surrounded by friends and family. Please feel free to call me if you ever need to talk.
>
> God bless,
> Peggy Say

Betty knew that Peggy was Terry Anderson's sister. *Why would she take the time to write to me? Her brother's been in there for years!* Betty was deeply moved by the note and tried to recollect whether she'd seen Peggy on television and what she looked like. *She must be a very kindhearted woman. I'll call her before Christmas. Or maybe I'll just write to her.*

Instead of putting the note in the pile of unanswered mail that was gathering dust on the left side of her desk,

Betty impulsively folded it and slipped it into her wallet. It gave her hope, somehow, and reminded her that her situation could be worse.

She woke up early the next morning and methodically put her luggage in the car. She found herself moving in slow motion. Silently she prayed, *Lord, if there's a call I'm supposed to get, let it come now, before I leave the house.*

What if Jon got out? What if they allowed him to telephone her on Christmas day and she didn't answer? Fear clashed with reason. She'd put her father's phone number on the outgoing recording "in case of emergency," and she had tested and retested the code for retrieving her messages. Jim and Joyce at OMI had agreed to check her mail every few days, in case some sort of communiqué came through from Lebanon. In short, there was no way Jon couldn't reach her.

I'm homesick and I haven't even left the driveway! She fought back tears, double-checked the front door lock and drove away.

The eighteen-hour drive to Medford, Oregon, was more enjoyable than she'd hoped. There was a certain peacefulness in the solitude. By the time she pulled up to Harold's mobile home, she was too tired to be concerned about anything but sleep.

Next morning she woke up in a small, tidy room. She knew Harold was up. He was sneezing, and every time he sneezed the whole structure shuddered slightly. *Talk about close quarters . . .* She got up, brushed her hair, and quietly dialed her home telephone number. "You have no messages," the mechanical voice reported.

As she entered the living room she was greeted by a blast of hot air. *Geez, it's like walking into a nuclear reactor.* An enormous wood stove glowed red, heating the room to an ungodly temperature. Beads of sweat broke out on her face as she sipped at the strong, scalding coffee her father poured for her.

"Daddy, it's got to be ninety degrees in here!" Harold Fuller had always been partial to warm indoor environments.

"It's cold outside! I'm heading out for more wood." Harold shuffled off in his bedroom slippers toward some unseen woodpile, and as the front door opened a welcome Arctic blast swept across the living room. He quickly returned, laden with firewood.

"Why don't you have a Christmas tree?"

"Trees are a waste of time and money," he grumbled, stacking the wood against the stove. There was an awkward pause. "Why, did you want a Christmas tree or something?"

"I thought I came up here for Christmas, Daddy." Betty looked at her father affectionately. He was a character, to be sure. "Of course I want a Christmas tree."

"What about that plastic one we used to . . ."

"Forget it!" she interrupted him without apology. "I'll get us a real tree. Where are we going to put our presents if we don't have a tree?"

"What presents?"

Betty sighed and shook her head. She looked around the room. It was cluttered with familiar objects that she remembered from childhood. But not a single Christmas decoration could be seen. *He probably misses Mother too much to celebrate Christmas.*

"Look, Daddy, if I get us a tree, do you think you can find our old boxes of ornaments?"

"Oh, they're probably out in the shed. Yeah, I'll find them but you'd better be careful—they're probably full of black widow spiders. Go ahead and get dressed. I'll take you into town and we'll look for a tree."

Harold was whistling an unidentifiable tune and stoking the fire yet again when Betty went into the little bathroom to take a shower. She located a thin, tattered bath towel and looked inside the shower stall. "Daddy, do you have anything besides Lava soap?" she shouted.

"What's wrong with Lava soap?" he shot back. "I think maybe I've got some Boraxo somewhere."

"Never mind . . ." Betty sighed again and rummaged around in her overnight case until she found a small bar of hotel soap. *This could be a very long, very hot visit,* she thought to herself. And then she smiled. In fact she almost laughed. On the wall of the bathroom was a miniature plaque that said in tiny pink letters,

BE STILL AND KNOW THAT I AM GOD

Harold Fuller wasn't about to pay for cable television, so Betty was without her faithful companion, CNN. The only thing she could tune in on her father's venerable radio was an annoying combination of static and country music—not one all-news station could be found anywhere on the dial. ABC's "World News Tonight" was her sole source of daily information. Jon seemed farther away from Oregon than from Los Angeles.

Days passed with a penetrating sameness. Finally, after an uneventful week had come and gone, Red Jeffrey appeared on Christmas Eve. He blew in with a mighty gust, bearing a foil-wrapped object under his arm.

"Venison," he announced as he dropped it on the table. Red was aptly nicknamed. His ruddy face was crowned with a ring of graying auburn hair. He wore a red-and-blue plaid wool jacket, jeans, and workman's boots.

"You're Betty? I'm Red. Got any coffee?"

A man of few words, Betty noted as she plugged in the percolator. She scrounged up some ancient, crumbling cookies, put them on a plate, and took them into the living room.

"It's hotter 'n hell in here, Fuller," Red complained, yanking off his jacket and unbuttoning the top two buttons of his flannel shirt.

Harold chuckled and glanced at Betty. He leaned back in his recliner and after a few USMC amenities said, "Well, Red, what can you tell us about the Beirut hostages?"

Red pulled out a handkerchief and mopped his brow. "Best bet for those suckers is a commando raid. Otherwise they're never gonna get out. That officer I told you about, Samuels, he says the city used to be crawling with CIA, but they've probably pulled out most of the agents by now. He says the federal government's washed its hands of the whole damned place. They've lost too much blood and screwed up too many times. Nobody wants to touch it."

Harold scowled. "So who'd stage a raid? Marines?"

"Delta Force, probably, if Bush approved it. But my guess is that the Israelis might like to win some points in this deal. I'm voting for that."

Is he speculating or does he know something? Betty studied Red's face. It was inscrutable. He was a career Marine, near retirement age. Who did he know? What had he heard? He and Harold had met when Red was "wet behind the ears," as Harold described it. For some unexplainable reason, the two men had remained in contact.

Betty wanted more details. "Red, what do you mean the government's washed its hands of the whole thing? Do you mean they aren't doing anything?"

"I mean that the hostages in Beirut aren't particularly high on anybody's list these days. Most people won't say it, but they're convinced that those guys never should have been in there in the first place. It's risky business."

"Jon was promised a Druze guard . . ." Betty said, feeling protective of Jon.

"Yeah, right. So was Terry Waite. The Druze are useless. Their warlord, Jumblatt, is a junkie. Why would anyone trust the Druze?"

Red looked at Betty as if she were a complete imbecile. In response, her voice grew sharply defensive. "How would an ordinary person know whether or not to trust the Druze? Jon was told by the people who hired him that they would protect him."

"Well, he should have done his homework before he trusted his life to them. No offense, but guys like your boyfriend put the old US of A in a terrible spot. They make foolish decisions, and then expect somebody else or the government to bail them out."

Betty was extraordinarily angered by Red's words, but for some reason she was even more enraged by his arrogance. "Look, Red. You don't know Jon. And you don't know any of the other hostages. How dare you sit there and criticize men who are chained to a wall somewhere, and . . ." Her voice was growing loud and shrill.

Red was perfectly capable of rising to the occasion. His face was more florid than ever. "Hey, little lady, don't you lecture me! I'm the one who'll end up bustin' his butt for some little ignoramus like your boyfriend."

Betty jumped up, grabbed her coat, and stormed out the door. The northern wind cooled her cheeks and ran soothing fingers through her hair. She was too incensed to think orderly thoughts. Red's insensitivity overwhelmed her. How could he sit there and blindly insult and practically assault the man she loved? Didn't he understand her grief? Her loss? *Oh, God. I would have been in London with Jon right now if this hadn't happened.* For a moment pain knifed through her chest and anguish blackened her senses.

She walked down one country road after another. Twilight was stretching long shadows across the landscape. Brittle ice was forming along the edge of puddles, and the stark silhouettes of pine trees stood black and tall against the silver sky. Her nose and lips were numb with cold. She thrust her hands deeply into her pockets.

What an obnoxious . . . but only obscenities came to mind. Red Jeffrey had managed to breathe new life into a couple of them.

The man's words rankled, to be sure. But beneath his cruel diatribe, Betty gradually realized some seeds of truth. Drifts of the same sentiment had come her way before, albeit never so harshly: Lebanese hostages were victims of their own poor judgment, or, worse yet, losers in a deadly gamble. As for the government's posture? Concern for the future of the hostages was expressed in effusive public statements, while in actual policy resolution of the predicament seemed to have been left to the winds of chance.

An even deeper issue troubled Betty, although she'd never mentioned it to anyone. Jon was neither fish nor fowl. He wasn't an American citizen, but he had an INS green card, which probably indicated to the New Zealand government that he really wasn't their concern, either. Did New Zealand have a hostage policy? Was it the same as Britain's? Was anyone anywhere concerned about Jon Surrey-Dixon's release besides Elisabeth Casey?

After a couple of hours of cooling off, literally and figuratively, Betty crunched her way up Harold's gravel driveway. Red's car was gone. She quietly opened the door. Was Harold upset with her for walking out? *Ask me if I care . . .* Betty was mentally repacking her bags.

"Hi, Betty. Did you have a good walk?" Harold had plugged in the lights on the little Christmas tree, plainly a conciliatory gesture. "Sorry about Red. He's a Marine, and that means he's got a mind of his own."

She sat down and looked at her hands, absently watching the reflected Christmas lights dance across her diamond. "Do you agree with what he said, Daddy?" *Because if you do, I'm leaving here, right this minute, Christmas or no Christmas.*

"Betty, I'll tell you how I feel. I think Jon is in God's hands. You know I'm not the Bible scholar your mother was, but I want to read you something I read this morning. I think it's something to hang onto for him."

Pages rustled as Harold fumbled through his well-worn Scofield Bible. His thick fingers tried to turn the delicate, gilt-edged pages. He cleared his throat, and read,

> I called upon the LORD in distress: the LORD answered me, and set me in a large place.
>
> The LORD is on my side; I will not fear; what can man do unto me?
>
> The LORD taketh my part with them that help me; therefore shall I see my desire upon them that hate me.
>
> It is better to trust in the LORD than to put confidence in man.
>
> It is better to trust in the LORD than to put confidence in princes.

"That's verses 5 through 9 of Psalm 118," he said as he raised his eyes and searched his daughter's face. Was she listening or had she tuned him out?

"Betty, you're going to hear a lot of opinions, a lot of rumors, and a lot of political nonsense as long as Jon's over there. And the fact of the matter is, there's nothing you can do except pray. And wait. And try not to blow your top." He closed his Bible, got up, and walked over to throw some more wood on the already raging, snapping fire.

"Daddy," she waited to see if she had his attention. She did. "You may not have bought me anything for Christmas, but you just gave me the best present ever."

Their eyes met, for once mirroring unhindered love and understanding. The moment was almost too much for Harold.

"What do you mean, I didn't buy you anything for Christmas?" he barked. "You'll get your presents tomorrow morning, just like you always did."

Betty returned home to piles of mail. Tired after the long drive from Oregon, she tried desperately to concentrate as she leafed through dozens of envelopes. A large manila one had come from the couple she'd met at Erica's dinner party. Doris and . . . what was his name? "The Walkers" said the return address.

The note read,

> Dear Betty,
>   Here are the things you'll need for the trip we promised you. We sincerely hope you'll find it to be an encouraging and helpful time. The gentleman whose card is enclosed will pick you up at the airport—he works for Henry's news service.

Henry . . . that's right. Henry and Doris.

Enclosed in the envelope, along with the note and the business card, were a United Airlines ticket to Washington, D.C. and a confirmation memo from One Washington

Circle Hotel. Betty was to leave January 6 and return four days later.

Jim Richards had agreed to take her to the airport. Just as they were going out the door, the telephone rang.

"Let it go . . ." Jim suggested. "We don't want to be late."

"I'll just see who it is . . ." Betty never ceased to imagine that Jon was somehow going to call her.

"Hello, is this Betty? This is Vince Angelo. Did you get my letter about Jon?"

Vince Angelo. Vince Angelo. Oh yes, the writer who was with Jon in Beirut.

"Yes, thanks, I did . . ."

"I'm calling you from Washington . . . D.C."

"Vince, as a matter of fact, I was just going out the door to catch a flight to Washington. How long will you be there?"

"The rest of the week. Where are you staying?"

"At One Washington Circle."

"Shall I call you there?"

"Yes. Of course. I'd love to talk to you."

After making the arrangements to meet, Betty hung up and headed out the door. Something troubled her about the call. For some reason she didn't want to hear the details of Jon's abduction. Yet, logically, she ought to be willing to sit down with the last person who saw Jon, to hear what he might have to say. She sighed loudly enough for Jim to notice.

"Betty, don't worry. You'll enjoy your time in Washington. It'll be good for you."

"Jim, all of this is so unreal. It's like a long, long nightmare. I don't want to go to Washington. I don't want to be on television. I don't want to talk about the hostages or think about the hostages or hear about the hostages. I just want to wake up and find Jon here, beside me."

Betty surprised herself by crying. In recent days tears had seemed to be forever spilling out of her eyes. She hadn't really laughed in weeks. And there was no relief in sight.

Catching her flight out of LAX, she dozed on and off during the flight. She awoke to find the aircraft banking over D.C. Although it was dark, she quickly recognized several buildings and monuments that were bathed in floodlights. The Jefferson Memorial. The Capitol building. The White House. An incurably proud American, Betty was exhilarated at the sight of such beloved landmarks.

I can't believe I'm here!

It was about 7:00 P.M. when she deplaned at National Airport. Betty scanned the crowd until she saw a young man holding up a sign bearing her name. She waved to him. "I'm Elisabeth Casey." He immediately took her bag and introduced himself. "I'm Derek Davis. Did Henry Walker by chance tell you that you're invited to a dinner tonight?"

"No, he just said you'd meet me."

"Well, it was sort of a last-minute decision. We happened to check with Peggy Say, and there's a dinner at a downtown restaurant for the hostage families. She's invited you to join them if you aren't too tired."

Betty was, in fact, exhausted. But she'd come all this way to meet the others. She was especially anxious to meet Peggy, and feeling slightly troubled that she'd not answered her kind note.

"I'll go," she said. "But I'd like to drop my stuff off at the hotel first, if it isn't out of the way."

"Not at all, Ms. Casey," Derek smiled at her, picked up her luggage, and they were on their way.

When they arrived at Le Petit Chat, a crowded café several blocks from the hotel, Derek led Betty to a woman whom she immediately recognized from television. Peggy Say glanced up, blew a plume of smoke over her shoulder, and smiled. "Hi, I'm Peggy."

"I'm Elisabeth Casey—from California." Betty extended her hand.

"Sit down! We're just talking about the usual insanity at the State Department. I'll introduce you once everybody's here."

Betty listened for the next two hours to an ongoing conversation that nearly left her breathless. Her not-so-positive reaction to George O'Ryan of the State Department had been mild compared to what she was hearing. Several hostage families were represented at the table, and not one of them could find a kind thing to say about O'Ryan.

"I think he's history," Peggy commented amidst clouds of blue-gray smoke. "I hear there are changes coming. There've been so many complaints about him, he's being transferred—out of the country."

"The farther away the better. Just as long as they don't replace him with another spook," someone muttered and everybody laughed.

Betty looked at Peggy in bewilderment. "What's a spook?"

"CIA. Be careful who you're talking to," she chuckled.

On and on the free-ranging conversation went. Betty listened as closely as possible. Most of these people had been at the heart of the Lebanon hostage crisis for years. They weren't afraid to name names disrespectfully, from the president of the United States on down. They weren't reluctant to criticize—even condemn—U.S. policy. They had survived Irangate, heard every excuse, seen every cover-up, and come up without their loved ones in the process. But, in spite of it all, they were able to laugh, even in the face of such horrendous circumstances.

The more Betty listened, however, the more unclear she was about one particular matter. Who was responsible for getting the hostages out? It sounded to her like the State Department was at odds with the Justice Department on the subject. And the Justice Department wanted no action whatsoever from the Defense Department. And, although the President seemed to be sincerely troubled about the matter, he was committed to no direct negotiations. Although a handful of congressmen were expressing continuing concern, Congress itself was irresolute on the subject.

Who was responsible for the hostages? Everyone, it seemed. And no one at all.

When the dinner ended, Betty shared a cab back to the hotel with Peggy. "I want to thank you for writing to me at Christmas. Betty pulled Peggy's handwritten message out of her purse. "I've been carrying it around with me since the day it arrived. I'm sorry I didn't answer. You wouldn't believe the pile of mail on my desk."

"Oh yes I would," Peggy laughed. She took Betty's hand and looked at her diamond. "I'm sorry about your wedding. But I have a feeling Jon will be out long before Terry is. You just hang in there."

"Why do you say that?"

"I think he's being held by a different group of captors, and they aren't as hardline as the guys who have Terry."

"How do you know?"

"I've been around this hostage business for a long time, Elisabeth . . ."

"Why don't you call me Betty."

Peggy nodded as she lit another cigarette. "I hear a lot, and I know a lot of people, Betty. You hang in there and keep praying. God's going to take care of both Jon and Terry. You've got to keep the faith, not just for your-self, but for Jon. Know what I mean?"

Betty nodded. She looked at Peggy in amazement. Again and again Peggy had ridden a heartless roller-coaster from soaring hope to crushing disappointment. She'd lost both her father and a brother since the kidnapping and was forever hearing the promise that Terry might possi-bly be coming out "this weekend." She had spent endless months and years waiting for a phone call that never came. And now, here she was, encouraging Betty to pray.

"You're a remarkable woman, Peggy," Betty hugged her as they said good night.

Peggy laughed. "Be in the lobby at nine-thirty. There's a hostage remembrance service at the Capitol building at ten. I'm going to have to leave town after that, but call me when you get home, okay?"

"Okay."

Betty unlocked her room, undressed, and got into her nightgown as quickly as possible. She clicked on the tele-vision, requested a wake-up call, brushed her teeth, and started to get into bed. Suddenly a peculiar thought struck her. Perhaps it was because her lower back was aching with fatigue. Or maybe it was inspired by the feminine hygiene product commercial that had just graced the tele-vision.

How long had it been since her last period?

Had she had one since Jon left?

Had she had one since . . .

She caught her breath. It had to have been at least six weeks. She stared at herself in the mirror, shivering with a new fear. Again, tears. Maybe she was emotional because . . .

Betty got on her knees beside the bed. Was this a night-mare within a nightmare? Did God care about her? "Keep the faith," Peggy had said.

Oh, Lord. Please. By now she was crying so hard that she could hardly speak. It had been many years since she had felt so utterly, helplessly alone.

Oh God. Don't let me be pregnant. I can't face it. It's too much. I can't go through something like that without Jon. And Lord, everyone will know. The whole world will know—I've been on every network, in every newspaper. Oh God, please. Help me, Lord!

Exhausted and frightened beyond words, she crawled into the bed, shivering and sobbing. In less than a minute's time she had fallen into a deep, dreamless sleep.

Next morning's prayer vigil at the Capitol building was a sweet, moving occasion sponsored by several humanitarian groups that had taken on the hostages as a special project. Music was performed, prayers were offered, and words of encouragement were spoken by several leading clerics, congressmen, and journalists. Betty was touched by the event but frequently distracted by the fear that had so unpleasantly introduced itself to her the night before.

Afterward, a brown-eyed man with a finely chiseled face and graying hair approached Betty. "Are you Elisabeth Casey?"

"Yes, I am," Betty eyed the man curiously.

"I'm a friend of Jon's"

"Oh, you must be Vince Angelo."

"No, I'm not Vince, but I know him. My name is Mike Brody, and I'm doing some work on the hostage situation. I wondered if you could spare a few minutes. I just want to ask you a few questions."

Why did Peggy say, "Be careful whom you talk to?" Was she serious?

"I'll help if I can."

"Let's sit down over here." Betty was glad to sit down. Her back was aching again. "Tell me, to your knowledge, did Jon have any contact with Lebanese nationals?"

"No, I don't think so. Jon had a last minute call to go on assignment there, and from what he said I don't think he'd been to Lebanon before."

Betty felt like an outsider in her fiancé's life, and even more so when Mike replied, "Yes, we know that he had been there before. We're just trying to piece some information together."

"What exactly do you do? Are you with the State Department?"

The man laughed disarmingly, quite prepared for her questions. "I work for the government, Elisabeth, and I do work in cooperation with State. We're all in this together—I'm sure you're aware of that."

"Mike," Betty tried to hide the defensiveness she felt. "I've known Jon for a couple of years, but he certainly hasn't told me everything about himself. There just hasn't been time, with all his traveling around."

"Well, Jon is a well-traveled man, and he's gotten acquain-ted with a lot of people around the world. I'm just interested in knowing whom he might have been planning to see in Beirut."

Betty was fascinated by Mike. She could quickly see that he was extremely intelligent. It seemed to her that he had something specific in mind—something he wasn't about to reveal. His eyes reflected an inner calm. He seemed to be very much in control of himself. And, for some reason, he made her want to talk to him.

"Mike, can I ask you something? Is anyone doing anything about getting Jon out?"

Mike smiled affably. "The hostages are a very important issue to the Bush administration, Elisabeth. More important than you might imagine. Clearly, a great deal is being done on their behalf. But past experience has taught this administration that it's best not to involve the families in any hostage release efforts. Emotion and good judgment don't always go hand in hand. Just ask Ronald Reagan."

Mike checked his watch and seemed surprised by what it said. "Look, if you'll excuse me, I've got to get going. If you come across any names or addresses Jon might have gathered in Beirut, give me a call."

Mike wrote his name and two phone numbers on a note pad, ripped it out, and handed it to her. Apparently, he didn't have a business card. "The second number is my home. Call anytime, day or night. Thanks for taking the time. Oh, by the way, that's Vince Angelo over there. Weren't you looking for him?"

Mike seemed to be in quite a rush, but he pointed out a small, balding man in his early thirties. Vince had a halo of curly black hair, a cherubic smile, and a nervous manner. Betty introduced herself to him.

"Betty! I was going to call you this afternoon!" Vince winked at her and spoke with a strong New York accent. "My you are a beauty, aren't you? Jon told me, but I didn't believe him."

"Thanks, Vince." Betty wasn't feeling particularly beautiful at the moment, and she seriously doubted his sincerity.

Don't come on to me, pal. I'm in no mood.

"Look, can I buy you lunch? I'd like to tell you a little bit about our trip." Vince was fidgeting with a pen, trying to attach it to a notebook.

They left the Capitol grounds, walked past the Supreme Court and toward Union Station. "Vince, do you know a man named Mike Brody?"

"Never heard of him." He was still struggling with the pen.

"That's funny. He knows you—he just pointed you out to me. He was asking me about Jon's friends in Lebanon."

Now she had his full attention. "Hmmm. Must be a spook. I don't know anybody named Brody. The only friends Jon mentioned to me were the Badr brothers. They were a couple of guys he'd met there on another assignment, from the Bekaa or somewhere. He thought they might help us find some good human interest stories."

"When was Jon in Beirut?"

"Probably in '82, during the Israeli invasion. But I'm not sure. In any case, I just wanted you to know that he talked about you all the time and was really excited about the wedding. The last thing he said, or shouted as they were taking him away, was 'Tell Betty I love her.'"

"He said that while they were taking him?" Betty's hands covered her face. Her eyes closed. She was trying very hard not to visualize a scene that might never again leave her mind.

"I heard him call it out while they were tying him up, before they gagged him. He was already blindfolded, and he just sort of shouted it toward us. He wanted one of us to tell you."

Betty was unable to speak. Nausea was creeping into her stomach. "You know, Vince," she finally said, "I'm not at all hungry. In fact I'm really not feeling well. Would you forgive me if I took a rain check on lunch?"

Vince looked at her sympathetically. She was white as a ghost. "I'll hail a cab and help you get back to your hotel safely. You must be emotionally exhausted."

Yeah, and pregnant.

"Thanks, Vince. That's nice of you. Is there anything else I should know about your time with Jon?"

Vince hailed a cab, and they both climbed into the back seat. "One Washington Circle," he instructed the driver. He turned to Betty, "Jon just said a lot of nice things about you, that's all. I guess I've never seen a man more in love."

"Well, I'm in love with him too. I just pray this story has a happy ending."

"Oh, they stopped murdering hostages years ago. He'll make it. By the way, did you say this Brody guy pointed me out to you?" By now Vince was fussing with a wad of dollar bills.

"Yes. He said, 'That's Vince Angelo.'"

Vince looked up at her sideways. "Was Jon messing around with the CIA, Betty?"

"Jon?"

They stared at each other blankly. In some ways, Vince knew more about Jon than she did. The fact was, she hadn't had time to really find out about his past. They had talked a lot about feelings, but very little about incidents. Maybe he was involved with the CIA. If so, would he have told her? Probably not.

The cab pulled up at the hotel. When she tried to pay, Vince wouldn't let her, peeling off several one dollar bills for the cabbie. "Thanks so much for tracking me down to tell me all that, Vince. I know Jon will appreciate it." He kissed her on the cheek as they parted.

She took the elevator to her room, kicked off her shoes, and collapsed on her bed. Why was she so tired? Was fatigue a symptom of pregnancy? Her back was still unusually sore and for that matter so were her breasts. She stared at the ceiling in horror, fear assaulting her from all directions.

Why was she marrying a man she didn't really know all that well? Was he some sort of a spy? Did he have a weird, secret life, carefully hidden from her? It was entirely possible, considering how little time they'd spent together.

Or, like her father's friend Red had said so unkindly, was Jon just an ignoramus—a foolish man who would trade his future with her for a dangerous job and a little excitement?

Was she about to marry a man who wasn't really the person she thought he was?

Worse yet, was she carrying his baby?

As the minutes passed all her uncertainties gave way to the echo of his words, shouted to anyone who might hear. "Tell Betty I love her." She loved him too, even in the midst of this present crisis, and longed to somehow convey that knowledge to him. There was an unexplainable link between them, no matter what transpired.

Will it last? The familiar question resurfaced in her thoughts.

This time, however, there was a reply. The still, small answer was unmistakable.

It's up to you.

4
____

*B*etty awoke feeling disoriented and depressed. She had slept fitfully—ambulance sirens approaching the hospital across the street had awakened her several times. And, once again, Jon's battered face had invaded her chaotic dreams.

Her lower backache continued, aggravated by a night of tossing and turning. Her breasts were still tender. She flipped on the television, trying to distract herself from all thoughts of pregnancy. A news anchorwoman reported:

A demonstration by a group of Christian fundamentalists intended to close down an abortion clinic in Southern California, was interrupted by police late yesterday. A spokesperson for Planned Parenthood said . . .

Off went the television. *Abortion clinics. That's just what I need to hear about. Planned Parenthood . . .*

Suddenly, a panic-inspired idea flashed. Impulsively, she grabbed the yellow pages out of a nightstand drawer.

Let your fingers do the walking, she grimly consoled herself as she leafed through the P's.

She dialed a number. The person who answered referred her to another number. She immediately called it.

"Yes. I'm interested in finding out if I'm pregnant. Can you help me?"

Her call was transferred to a counselor. Quite unrehearsed, Betty blurted out, "It's been six weeks since my last period, my boyfriend's away for an extended time and I'm afraid I'm pregnant."

"We can schedule an appointment for you today, Miss, if you'd like to come in."

"If I am pregnant, do you, uh . . ."

"We can discuss your options when you come in."

"If I were to want an abortion, would I be able to do it today?"

"I'll have to check our schedule. Probably so, but first let's find out whether you need one. What is your name?"

"Uh . . . Fuller. Beth Fuller."

"Okay, Beth. Can you be here at 11:00 A.M.?"

"Do I need to bring anything with me in case we go ahead with the . . ."

"No, it's an out-patient procedure. Just be sure someone is with you to drive you home."

"I'll be coming in a cab. Will you take an out-of-state check?"

"Yes, of course. We'll see you at eleven."

Betty hung up, her thoughts racing. *I'll just get it over with and think about it later. God, I'm sorry, but I can't face this. I know You'll forgive me. It's just too much.*

She checked the clock. It was 9:00 A.M. This time tomorrow she'd be on a plane home. Or would she? Could she fly less than twelve hours after an abortion? *I don't dare ask them. They'll say no.*

Betty paced around the room. She opened the sliding glass door and looked out at the passersby strolling along the sidewalk below. *Nobody knows. Nobody cares.* She slid the door back in place and clicked the lock. Absent-mindedly, she made herself a cup of coffee in the little kitchenette.

Some people say it's murder. Is it murder?

She plopped herself in a chair, spilling the coffee on her nightgown.

It's a late period, that's all. Just a late period. I wouldn't murder a baby, but I'd go to the ends of the earth to start my period about now.

Two things troubled Betty. Although the morality of abortion had never been of interest to her, she knew very well that some people were wild-eyed fanatics about the subject. Did they know something she didn't? Her thinking process was riddled with confusing fears, but she still had enough presence of mind to wonder just what it was she was about to do.

The other matter was a practical one. What if she was bleeding heavily tomorrow morning? Or in intolerable pain? Or faint and sick to her stomach? She had to use that ticket to get home—it was unchangeable, nonrefundable. And the last thing she wanted to tell Doris and Henry Walker was that she had to pay an extra fare to take a later flight because of a trip to an abortion clinic.

God, I'm so scared. I'm so scared.

She took a shower and got dressed. It was 10:00 A.M. by the time she was ready to go. Conflicting thoughts raged in her mind. Religious thoughts. Logistical thoughts. Romantic thoughts. Sentimental thoughts. Tough-minded thoughts. Sorrowful thoughts.

I need to talk to someone. Not a single person came to mind. Only Jon and how dearly she needed to be in his arms.

If only . . .

She scribbled the clinic address on a hotel notepad, grabbed her purse, and rushed out the door. It was a little too early for her to go to the clinic, but she was far too restless to stay in her room. She strode determinedly into the elegant hotel lobby. "Good-bye, Ms. Casey, have a good morning," the woman at the desk said cheerily."

"Can I get a cab for you?" said the doorman.

She nodded.

He motioned to a waiting taxi.

"Where are you going, Miss?"

"Uh," she glanced at her watch and at the crumpled paper in her hand. "I'll explain when I get in the car."

He nodded, smiled, and closed the door behind her.

"Yes mum?" said the cab driver, who had a heavy East Indian accent.

She paused. Looked at the paper. Looked out the window. Should she go to the clinic now? Should she go at all . . . ever? Betty fought off some new tears, and shook her head sadly and in resignation.

Jon's baby. It's all I have left of him. I can't go through with it . . . Finally she said, "Take me to the Smithsonian, please."

"Yes, mum. The Smithsonian. You will like it very much, Mum. I think you will spend the whole day there."

Betty looked out the window again and then at the cabbie's kind face in the rear-view mirror. "I'm sure you're right. I'll probably stay there all day."

Next morning, as Betty was checking out of her room, the clerk at the desk handed her an envelope. Inside she found a silver-colored bracelet, bearing Jon's name and the date of his kidnapping. It also bore the inscription "Hebrews 13:3." An enclosed note said that it had been left for her by a representative of some organization called Friends in the West.

"It's a prayer bracelet," the note explained. "Hebrews 13:3 says 'Remember those in prison as if imprisoned with them.' We want you to know that the hostages are being remembered in prayer by people all over the world who are wearing these bracelets.

"I'm sorry I couldn't give you the bracelet in person, but I have to be in Virginia today and tonight. In any case, be assured that you are not alone."

The note had obviously been written in a rush and the signature was indecipherable. Betty squinted at the name—it looked like it began with an L. The rest was a scribble. Finally she shrugged. *What difference does it make? It's the thought that counts.*

And it was a kind thought, to be sure. But beyond the significance of the bracelet, which she immediately squeezed around her left wrist, a single phrase from the note meant more to Betty than anything else.

". . . you are not alone."

Never in her life had she felt more alone. God, Who had been a close companion during some of her most painful days, seemed remote and even nonexistent. It occurred to her that while other difficulties had been thrust upon her without her consent, this set of circumstances was different. This time she could claim responsibility. This time she had done "something wrong."

Whatsoever a man soweth, that shall he also reap." Lucilla had enthusiastically quoted that inflexible little passage a few hundred times when various church folk and relatives got trapped in their own tangled webs of misbehavior.

Oh, yes, Betty had heard all about the unconditional love of God. But she'd rarely had the heart to believe in it. The love she had experienced in her childhood had been conditioned on good behavior. Betty could not grasp the fact that any love, especially from a righteous, holy God, could be forgiving and unchanging, no matter what she did.

She glanced at the note again. "... you are not alone." She clung to the phrase as if it were some mystical fortune-cookie message from heaven. Could God remain beside her through a time like this? He'd seen her through a divorce, and that was pretty disreputable. But this? This was inexcusable.

At least I didn't have an abortion.

When Betty left the hotel, the doorman hailed a cab and helped the driver with the luggage. Tipping him as he helped her into the taxi, Betty smiled more than a little appreciation to him for helping her change her mind the day before.

The cab driver artfully maneuvered them from the hotel to National Airport. Betty fingered the bracelet absentmindedly. She'd seen enough of Washington. Fortunately her plane was on time.

As she took her seat and buckled in, the lyrics of an old hymn drifted across her mind. It was the same hymn she'd remembered while driving home from Erica's house weeks before.

> The protection of His child and treasure
> Is a charge that on Himself He laid ...

Betty knew she was God's child, at least theologically. But His treasure? Surely He only tolerated her. Naturally He had real treasures—missionaries and ministers and sweet Christian housewives who'd never done anything wrong in their lives. But she was no treasure to God.

Or maybe the hymn itself was wrong. Maybe some dewy-eyed poet had warped the One True God into a sentimental Grandpa. Surely He was more the way she thought of Him—stern, detached, generally disapproving.

A bit like Mother, she couldn't help but think. *And even if He loves me in some obligatory, cosmic sense, I sure can't imagine Him liking me very much. That's going way too far.*

She slept most of the way home, getting up stiffly to stretch and use the restroom before the final approach to LAX imprisoned her in her seat. She emerged from the cramped toilet facility with but one thought in her mind, and a joyous thought it was.

I'm not pregnant! Oh, thank you Lord. I'm not pregnant.

She wanted to stand up in the plane and shout out the news to all the passengers. Fortunately she didn't. She simply buckled her seat belt, rested her forehead on her right palm, and smiled quietly.

It must have been stress that delayed it. No wonder my back was aching—it always aches two days before I start my period. And naturally my breasts were sore and I've been crying. PMS—I've had PMS for almost three weeks!

She took a deep breath, and then another.

Oh God, thank you. Thank you. Thank you!

God had rescued her from her guilt again. Did that mean her time of intimacy with Jon was all right with Him? Or did it simply mean He was gracious and forgiving? Perhaps He was being especially kind to her because of Jon's predicament.

After all, God is just, and Jon is being unjustly held. It's really unfair—unbelievably unfair. Maybe that kind of thing bothers God more than our everyday behavior. Maybe Jon's captivity even makes Him sad!

There was that kindhearted, compassionate God again. In spite of her skepticism, some words of verse started drifting around in Betty's mind, and she jotted them down before she forgot them.

The eyes of God have seen us,
And He's smiled through His tears.

Jim Richards met her at the gate, and she quickly
noticed that he'd brought Joyce Jiminez along. Their
familiar faces were a welcome sight, to be sure. Prolonged
hugs were lovingly exchanged.

"How are you, Betty? How was your trip?"

"I feel like I've been to Mars."

"Why? Was it that bad in Washington?"

"No, it's just that good to see you! Look what someone gave me!" She held out her left wrist, displaying the
prayer bracelet.

"How wonderful! I'd like one myself," Joyce
responded enthusiastically. "Did you meet with some of
the other family members?"

"I met all kinds of people. It was exciting. Exhausting.
And I'm ready to be in my own house with my own
chair!"

"Have you heard the news?" Jim glanced at her.

"What news?" Betty stiffened.

"There are some rumors about a hostage being released
in the next two weeks or so."

"Who says?" She was electrified.

"Some Arabic-language newspaper in Beirut is reporting an unnamed source close to the kidnappers as saying
that a release is imminent. Of course your phone is probably ringing off the hook again."

"Do you think it's true?" Betty searched his face for a
clue, for an expression of hope or encouragement.

Jim was silent for a few moments. He shook his head
and finally responded, "I've been thinking about this all
day, Betty. I think these rumors cause more heartache

than anything else. Let's just try to ignore it until we hear something more substantial."

"What do I say to the media?"

"Tell them you plan to keep praying, keep hoping, and keep waiting for Jon to come home."

Once inside her condo, Betty checked her answering machine. It hadn't had a single message when she'd accessed it remotely from Washington the night before. Now the light reported eighteen messages.

She listened to them, one by one. This time she didn't bother to write down the numbers. *They'll call back if they want me badly enough.*

Her trip to Washington had educated her about journalists. To most of them she was simply a sound bite. Or a paragraph in an assigned story. They were using her. In exchange for their intrusion, they shared tidbits of inside information with her, information that stirred her emotions but served no practical purpose in her life.

It was possible that certain international news shows were broadcast into Beirut. And the captors might, on the odd occasion, allow the hostages to see or hear reports about their own imprisonment. But as far as most newspapers and local broadcasts were concerned, the assignment editors needed Betty a lot more than she needed them.

Toward the end of the tape, a peculiar message caught her attention. It began with a fuzzy sound, punctuated by high-pitched beeps. Then a Middle Eastern voice said, "This is Abdul Badr calling from Lebanon. I wish to speak to you about your . . ." Click. The fuzzy sound returned, along with the beeps. It was cut off by the next call, another reporter's request for comment for the *San Diego Union*.

Betty listened to the Badr message again and again. Who would be calling her from Lebanon? How would he have gotten her number? What did he want? What should she do?

There's nothing I can do anyway, without a number. Even the name is hard to understand. Sounds like Badr. Isn't that the name of the brothers Vince Angelo mentioned? Should I call Mike Brody?

She looked for Brody's number among all the little scraps of paper in her purse. There was the abortion clinic address. There was Derek's business card. Finally she found it—she remembered the 703 area code. *Must be in Virginia,* she reasoned as she dialed the number.

"DDI," a woman's voice said.

"I . . . I'm trying to locate Mike Brody."

"Brody's at lunch. Can I have him call you?"

"I'll call him later. Thanks."

"DDI." I wonder what that means. I guess they wouldn't answer the phone "CIA."

She tried to dismiss the strange phone call from her mind, listlessly unpacking her bags and putting her toiletries away. Despite the emotional ups and downs, the crises and the visibility, it was during these times of hollow silence that her separation from Jon felt the most painful.

She suffered the most when the phone never rang, when day-after-day life merely went on without him. She missed far more than Jon's embrace, although that yearning most enticed her when she was troubled. But she longed to talk to him. To share her days with him. To have fun together.

The world was gray and empty without him. Reason told her that she should get on with her existence, busy herself, and leave Jon's plight to the experts. Of course she should pray, and pray she did. But it seemed that her best course of action would be to disconnect, somehow, from the whole problem. Unfortunately, such a response was impossible, at least for Betty, who carried Jon Surrey-Dixon around in her heart like a gold ingot—priceless but too heavy to bear.

The phone startled her repeatedly. For the next two hours she listened to the various voices through her answering machine. She'd heard most of them before. They simply wanted to invite her to utter something hostage-wise into a microphone. What could she say that she hadn't said before? *They're just doing their job, I guess. But thank God for answering machines.*

Later on that afternoon she heard Jim Richards' familiar voice. "Betty, are you there? Can you pick up the phone?"

She did.

"Betty, I realize you're supposed to be taking a leave of absence, but I'm sure you can't go on forever without a paycheck. I've got a Uganda project here I could use your help with. What do you think?"

"Oh, Jim. My mind is just obsessed with Jon. Do you think I can concentrate?"

"I think it's worth a try. In fact, I have a feeling it might be good for you. Why don't you finish out the week at home and then come in on Monday morning. Your desk is still empty, you know."

Sadder than ever, she hung up. It seemed disloyal to Jon to go back to work. And yet Jim was right. Financially she had to do something soon. Her phone bills alone were astronomical. What few book royalties she'd earned over the past two years certainly weren't going to cover her mortgage payments. She could never have made the trip to Washington if it hadn't been for the generosity of the Walkers.

That reminds me. I have to call them.

Henry answered the phone. "Well I'm glad we were able to help. Derek said you got to spend some time with Peggy Say. How was everything?"

"It was great. Thanks so much, Henry. It was an invaluable trip. I can't even tell you how much I learned. I only wish I could repay you."

"Well, let's put it this way, when Jon gets out, if he is willing to give our news syndicate an exclusive interview, it would be wonderful."

Betty considered his request. In all fairness, it was a reasonable exchange—her costly trip was every bit as important to her as any future interview might be to Henry Walker. Besides, it was up to Jon anyway.

"Of course, I can't speak for Jon, Henry. That's his decision, but I'll certainly put in a good word for you! Thanks again for your kindness."

"It was our pleasure. And we'll be in touch, Betty, not only by phone but in our prayers."

Betty hung up and sat motionless in the quiet of the room.

Nice people. Nice gesture. Nice to be alone.

She was still enjoying the blessed relief of her in-flight discovery when she remembered the words she'd written on the plane. She pulled them out of her purse and began to work on them.

Sounds more like a song than a poem, she commented to herself as she wrote. When it was finished, she recopied it on a blank sheet of paper. *Maybe I'll send it to Jon. Wouldn't it be wonderful if it miraculously reached him?*

First came the smile, then came the laughter—
"Hello! Here's my heart. Now we must say good-bye."
Night follows day, fall ends the summer,
We love and we wait—wait and we don't know why.
Lands and oceans come between us,
People, places, months, and years,
But the eyes of God have seen us,
And He's smiled through His tears.
He knows the way, He has the answer,
Somehow, some day, we'll never say good-bye.

The phone aroused Betty from a sound sleep early the next morning. "Hello, Elisabeth? Mike Brody here. I just wanted to touch base with you."

"Did you know I called you yesterday?"

"Nicole told me a woman called. Was it you? How are you, anyway?"

Why did she instinctively like this man whom she so thoroughly mistrusted?

"Oh, Mike, I'm fine. I called, but the reason was probably silly. I had a message on my answering machine from someone in Lebanon. The man got cut off, so I can't call him back because he didn't have a chance to leave a number." She paused. "By the way, you can call me Betty if you want."

"Thank you, Betty. Look, as far as returning that call is concerned, you'll have a hard time getting through to Lebanon anyway. There are hardly any lines. It's easier for them to call out. Did you get his name?"

"Yeah, it was something like Badr. Abdul Badr, I think."

"Anything else?"

"Well, I . . ." *How much should I tell this guy?*

"What else did he say?"

At least he's trying to do something, or he wouldn't be asking questions.

"Well, he didn't say anything else. But I think Vince Angelo told me that Jon knew some brothers in Lebanon with that last name, Badr. Or something like that. I'm really not sure."

"Did he say where these brothers live?"

"Is there someplace called Bawcaw?"

"You mean the Bekaa Valley?"

"Yes, I think that's it. That sounds right."

There was a brief pause. Mike was apparently writing down the information, perhaps even weighing it.

"Do you think it might be important, Mike?"

Mike laughed, again disarming her. "Everything's important, Betty. Anything we can learn about the situation can be helpful. Thanks for being so cooperative. Everyone I talk to isn't as pleasant as you. Call me any time!"

She hung up and the phone rang again almost immediately. This time she answered it without screening it. Again she heard the fuzzy sound, the high-pitched beeps. "Hello? Hello?"

There was a bothersome echo on the line. Betty's voice replayed in her ears every time she spoke.

"Is this Elisabeth Casey?"

"Yes? Who is this?"

"This is Abdul Badr in Lebanon. Can you hear me?"

"I can. Go ahead."

"Your friend is my friend too. I want to help you. Do you understand?"

"I . . . Yes. How can you help?"

"I have some information that may interest you. Let us say that your friend is visiting acquaintances of mine."

The man seemed to be choosing his words with great care. She had heard something in Washington about the phones being tapped in Lebanon. She decided to be careful too.

"Do you know where these people live?"

"Yes, they live nearby."

"What kind of information do you have?"

"I cannot discuss it on the telephone with you. I need to meet with you."

"Meet with me? I'm not coming there!"

"Perhaps we could meet in Europe. There may be some, how you say, expenses for me. But I will try."

"Then you will call me back?"

"I call, yes."

"Is Jon . . . is my friend all right?" Betty's eyes filled with tears.

"He is good, very good. I call you, yes?"

"Thank you."

Hope surged within Betty, quickly followed by ripples of suspicion. She immediately called Brody and related the conversation to him. She concluded her report with a question: "What do you think, Mike?"

Mike chuckled. "Well, from what I've learned, there are a lot of people in Lebanon who have some kind of information about the hostages. They may be related to someone who guards them. Or they may have gone to school with some of the kidnappers. These are the people who leak stories to newspapers—for a fee, of course. And they are the ones who help fill in the gaps for our intelligence people."

"But they really can't help that much?"

"Well I'm sure you'd agree that there isn't a whole lot anyone can do apart from quiet diplomacy, enormous ransom payments, or an all-out rescue mission."

"How would these people get my phone number?"

"It's not that difficult. Most of the news agencies have it, don't they?"

"Yes, they sure do. Every newspaper and television station in the country must have it."

"Well, there you go. Look, let me check this name out and I'll be in touch. Thanks again, Betty. You're a gem, you know that?"

She had a sudden afterthought. "Mike, do you know anything about an imminent hostage release?"

"It's from an unreliable source, Betty. Don't get your hopes up. Take care now and have a good day."

Betty smiled as she hung up the phone. Whether she wanted to admit it or not, she enjoyed talking to Mike Brody. For one thing, he was the first person she'd met, apart from the hostage families and her friends, who appeared to be even mildly concerned about the captives. Besides, he was an attractive man who thought she was nice. Whatever the case, Betty felt better after conversing with him.

She automatically turned on the television. After a few other stories, the one she was waiting for replayed.

"An imminent hostage release is being predicted by some sources in Lebanon," the anchorman said. "An unconfirmed report in a Beirut newspaper states that at least one hostage will be released by sundown Sunday."

Betty tried not to get too excited, but it was impossible not to dream. She called her father. "Daddy, have you heard the news?"

"Yeah, I heard. And I've been hearing the same thing for years." Harold hadn't missed a newscast in two decades. Even without CNN he managed to stay painfully well-informed.

"What do you mean?"

"I mean these rumors get started every few months

and nothing ever comes of 'em. You better turn off the TV and go look up that Psalm I read you at Christmas. You'll learn a lot more from that than from some cock-eyed raghead newspaper."

Betty's return to Overseas Ministries International felt like a mixed blessing, more good than bad. She had to tear herself away from her telephone every morning, from the oft-fantasized call that never really came. Naturally, she'd included OMI's phone number on her outgoing message just in case "the call" actually materialized. Meanwhile, she had to get out of bed, get dressed, and be at the office on time. This required more self-discipline than she cared to exercise some mornings.

But all in all it was good to be back among caring people, most of whom she dearly loved. She was soon busy on Jim's new project—an orphanage report about Uganda. As she worked on it, her memories often carried her back to Kampala, to the hot, humid days and the charcoal-scented nights of that equatorial city. She hadn't fully recognized it while it was happening, but she and Jon had first fallen in love in Kampala two years before, while working on a book together. The memory of those days was bittersweet indeed.

Maybe some day we'll go back there together, she tried to tell herself. *And next time, we'll be married. I'd love to see those precious children again. How they must have grown!* It seemed like an eternity since she first traveled there to meet Jon.

Her trusty OMI typewriter had been replaced by a brand spanking new computer. Friday morning she was trying to simultaneously compose her report, remember word processing commands, and not lose any important thoughts in the bowels of the machine. A frown of intense concentration was etched across her forehead. Mercifully the phone rang.

"Elisabeth, this is Claire Evans at ABC television. Sorry to track you down at work, but I'd like to schedule a guest appearance for Sunday afternoon if possible. Can you appear on our 'Pacesetters' broadcast? We're going to be featuring two or three individuals who are working their way through a crisis."

Betty had grown weary of television appearances, but she couldn't think of a logical excuse. "Um . . . what time do I have to be there?"

"Two-thirty. We'll send a limo to pick you up. I understand you're a writer. If you've written anything about your fiancé's captivity, we'd like to have you bring it."

"Well, yes, I do have a poem."

"Wonderful. That's just the kind of thing we want."

Betty shrugged. "Okay, why not? What time will the limo be at my house?"

"Two P.M. Please don't wear blue or white, and no busy patterns."

"I know. Thanks, Claire."

"Thank you, Elisabeth."

Jim walked in the door just as she hung up. "Who was that?"

"Oh, it was ABC television. They want me to be on 'Pacesetters'. Have you seen it?"

"Yes, I think so. It's personality profiles or something, isn't it?"

"It's sort of a *People* magazine on the air, I guess. Anyway I told them I'd do it, although I'm not sure why I said yes."

"It can't hurt to ask people to pray for the hostages, Betty."

"I guess you're right. It can't hurt a thing."

Sunday afternoon Betty dressed herself in her usual "television suit." It was taupe wool, this time accented with a jade green scarf. Betty examined herself in the mirror. Her face seemed to be aging from moment to moment. Every day more tiny lines seemed to be forming around her eyes, beneath which were ubiquitous dark circles.

Jon won't even want me when he sees me, she thought to herself, only half in jest. *This ordeal is taking its toll.*

Santa Ana winds had blown all the pollution out of the L.A. basin, and as the black limo cruised down the Pasadena Freeway, she couldn't help but enjoy the fresh, breeze-blown scenery. The skyline of Los Angeles soared upward against a brilliant blue sky. Freeways wound around like endless serpents, bejeweled with colorful vehicles.

Jon would love this day. Again the almost physical pain of missing him stabbed at her chest and rose in her throat. She fought it off. It was a futile sensation.

The studio was situated in Hollywood on Prospect Avenue. Betty was escorted into a dressing room, where a rather effeminate makeup artist bustled around theatrically. "God, what marvelous cheekbones!" he gushed, wielding a massive puff and sending billows of face powder heavenward.

The two other guests on the show were in the backstage "Green Room" when Betty walked in. One was the husband of a woman who had been on a life-support system for five years. The other was a woman whose husband was MIA in Vietnam. She spoke to them politely, wishing desperately she had stayed home.

What could she possibly say in response to any questions? She didn't want to talk about politics. She didn't know anything about Middle East affairs. Her personal life was nonexistent since Jon's kidnapping. All she could do was parrot Harold Fuller's orders: "Pray, wait and don't blow your top."

"Be sure and look at the camera, not at Mr. Phillips, even when he's asked you a question," an officious production assistant warned. Marvin Phillips, the host-interviewer was a benign sort of television personality who seemed genuinely concerned about each person he spoke to—until the cameras were off and he and his smile vanished without a trace.

The MIA wife was eloquent. She had done an admirable job of preparing her discussion about the Pentagon's apparent cover-up of Southeast Asian MIA and POW evidence. She was obviously angry, but self-controlled. And she made a strong case for the independent investigation that she felt needed to be launched. "I want my husband back!" she said firmly through almost clenched teeth.

The audience roared its approval.

The husband of the dying woman spoke simply but powerfully about the ethics of euthanasia and about his own feelings toward his wife. "You always hope for a miracle," he explained quietly. "Even when they say there're no brain waves and no hope for recovery, you just never know what might happen. You always remember what she was like in the old days, before she got sick. I'm not pulling no plug, Mr. Phillips, I'll tell you that."

Again, the audience responded enthusiastically.

"Elisabeth Casey's fiancé is a hostage in Lebanon. As I'm sure you know, he was kidnapped just days before their wedding last November. We all watched while this little lady's world suddenly fell apart."

Phillips paused to ask Betty a couple of rather superficial questions, which she answered without elaboration.

"Now nearly three months have gone by since the tragic interruption of your beautiful love story. So tell me,

Elisabeth, as a writer are you able to express your pain in words? Have you been able to write about your fiancé or your feelings?"

Betty found herself looking directly at Phillips, forgetting the production assistant's instructions.

"Well, yes, I've written a poem . . ."

Out of the corner of her eye, she saw someone wildly motioning for her to look at the camera. Awkwardly, she turned her head. It seemed unnatural and impolite not to be talking to Phillips when he was talking to her.

"Would you read it for us?"

Betty was obviously nervous. Now where should she look? At the paper, of course. She had to read the words—no way would she remember them in front of a live audience. She was extremely uncomfortable and wished with all her heart that she were home or suddenly invisible or otherwise missing in action herself. Nevertheless, she began to read.

"First came the smile, then came the laughter . . ." She read the few verses without a great deal of animation. She set the paper down in her lap when she finished. The audience was silent for a moment, as if they weren't quite sure whether she was finished or not. Finally a smattering of applause began just as the director cut to a commercial.

I never meant for anyone but Jon to hear it anyway! She tried to soothe herself in the face of such a frosty audience response.

"Thank you, you were all wonderful!" Phillips beamed and glowed. With the help of the crew, the three guests found their way out of the glaring lights and away from the crowd.

Never again! Betty vowed angrily to herself. *Never again will I subject myself to this kind of embarrassment.*

She felt like a runner-up in a talent show—a failed amateur. She chided herself for being such an absolute fool, for having exposed her most personal thoughts to the world at large. What did anyone really care about her heartaches? In that humiliating moment, as far as she could see, the people in the "Pacesetters" audience were nothing but bored voyeurs trying to inject some sort of intensity into their mundane lives.

Without a word, she gathered her belongings and all but crawled back to the limousine, grateful for its smoked glass windows. She coldly thanked the driver when she got home and unlocked the door to the sound of the ringing phone. She grabbed the receiver before the machine could pick up the call. *Maybe it's good news.*

"Hello?"

"Hello, is this Elisabeth Casey?"

"Yes, it is," she sighed. Once again "the call" had turned out to be an inquiring stranger.

"Ms. Casey, I'm Brian Demetrius. I'm with a band called ShakeDown. I just heard you read some lyrics on Marvin Phillips' show."

"Yes, I just got home from there."

"Would you consider letting us work on a tune to go with your lyrics? You may not have heard of us, but we've had two singles hit the charts in the last two years, and we want to do something for a humanitarian cause. Somebody up there's been looking out for us, you see, and this is our way of saying thank you."

"I don't understand what you want to do with the song. What would be humanitarian about it?"

"Oh, I'm sorry. I didn't make myself clear. We'd like to dedicate the song to the hostages in Lebanon and give a percentage of the proceeds to some of the organizations that are trying to help them. How would you feel about letting us use your lyrics? You'd make some money on the deal. And who knows, maybe your boyfriend will hear the tune played in his cell. They get to listen to music sometimes, I think."

"Well, I can't think of any reason to say no. What kind of music do you play anyway? 'ShakeDown' sounds pretty wild to me."

Brian named a couple of songs Betty had never heard of. Then he mentioned another—a song she actually liked very much. "You guys did that?"

"That's us!"

"I guess I never noticed the name of the band. So do you want me to mail these words to you?"

"Do you have a fax?"

"I can fax them to you tomorrow morning from my office."

"Great. Put your address on there too. Our attorney will be sending a contract. Thanks a lot, Elisabeth."

Betty was utterly drained when she hung up the phone. She collapsed in her chair in a weary daze, staring at the diamond on her hand. She loved the way light played with it, forever striking a different facet and surprising her with an unexpected burst of color. The effect was almost hypnotic, and she was exceptionally sleepy.

When she woke up, it was three o'clock in the morning. To her surprise, she was still wearing her television suit and jade green scarf.

This kind of thing has got to stop. I have to go to work tomorrow!

Clumsy with fatigue, she undressed, washed the makeup off her face, and gratefully slipped into bed. Just before sleep captured her again, she spoke aloud the three-word prayer that never really left her mind.

"God, deliver Jon," she murmured, vaguely aware

that the weekend was over and no hostages had been released.

Simultaneously, halfway around the world in a dark, sunless room another prayer was spoken aloud. It was offered up by a man who had all but lost his faith and yet continued to pound on the gates of heaven anyway.

"God, take care of Betty," Jon whispered. "Keep her safe. Give her rest. And please, whatever else You do, keep her loving me."

Jon's prayer was being answered even as he prayed. Unfortunately, he had no way of knowing.

5

_____

Betty was slouching over her desk, scratching out a bitter little verse on the back of an envelope. She read it sullenly, and then copied it onto her desk calendar.

> No, Hope.
> I will find another bridge
> From here to reality.
> I dare not set foot
> Upon your treacherous, unstable span.
> I do not trust you.

Despite various media predictions, the weekend had passed without a hostage release. Jim Richards had cautioned her. Her father had warned her. Even Mike Brody had been uncharacteristically direct in saying that rumors were just that—rumors.

So why was it that Betty had allowed hope to creep into some corner of her consciousness and her better judgment? And now came another inevitable Monday

morning, and with it the usual letdown. Thick, gray hope-
lessness clouded her thoughts. Certainly she was
exhausted from an unusually stressful Sunday. But the
real problem was a lingering, chronic depression that had
never really abated since the early November morning
call from George O'Ryan.

Betty tried to rouse herself out of her lethargy to stim-
ulate her lagging interest in the Ugandan orphanage
project that cluttered her desk. Untidy stacks of research
materials, photographs, and statistical printouts littered
every inch of her workspace. Very little of that information had as yet found its way into her report.

To make matters worse, Jim Richards had startled her
earlier this morning by saying, "I have a feeling we're
going to have to send you to Africa before this project is
over. We really don't have enough stories about individ-
ual children, and we'll never get them unless you go.
Everyone out there is just too busy to get the job done."

Panic seized her. There was no way she could go to
Uganda until Jon was free. Any kind of communication
was impossible there. Jon could be out on the street for
days before she'd know about it. The orphanage had no
phone, no radio, no television. Overseas calls from the
Kampala post office could take as long as two or three
hours to connect.

*I will absolutely not go to Uganda—not until Jon gets home.
And that's final,* she vowed to herself. It annoyed her that
Jim was insensitive enough to suggest such a thing. Didn't
he understand that the telephone and television were her
only remaining links with Jon?

Oh, there was God of course. But that particular spiritual link seemed more like a frayed string than a
trustworthy cable. Sure, He'd healed her skin years before.
And He'd helped her through the pregnancy scare. And

He'd taken care of her financially as long as she could remember. But what about the one thing that mattered the most? What about Jon? Their love, their marriage, their life together?

Never in her life had Betty questioned God's sovereignty. She had a strong belief in His right to do what He wanted with His children. This conviction was rooted in her familiarity with the Old Testament Book of Job and her own somewhat Job-like existence in years gone by.

When phones were ringing, unique opportunities were arising and people were reaching out in encouragement, Betty could envision some obscure divine purpose in it all. But days of unbroken silence were totally disabling. For the first time in her life, circumstances were eroding the core of her faith. She wasn't just questioning God's love this time. She was seriously wondering about the reality of His existence. He seemed out of touch, out of reach, and His absence left an aching void in her heart.

Day after day, week after week, life marched on, cruel and disinterested. Even at OMI, where everyone knew and loved Jon, it seemed that he was all but forgotten. And Betty sensed that some of her coworkers were hiding a private disapproval of her heavy heart.

She suspected that, to them, a "victorious Christian" would have handled the crisis quite differently. There would have been a sunny smile. Staunch words of faith and victory. A song of praise, extolling "peace in the midst of pain." *I've heard every Christian platitude that exists,* she sighed, staring across the parking lot at a gray-green bank of smog. Thick haze obscured the graceful San Gabriel mountains that normally reigned over the valley.

She let out a sigh and booted up her computer. It was time to stop all this philosophizing and get busy. Uganda. Kampala. Orphans.

Her mind was blank.

I'm supposed to care about orphans? Haven't I got enough troubles of my own?

How could the phone be so silent? Was anyone in the world thinking about Jon besides her? In Washington D.C.? In Wellington, New Zealand? What about heaven?

She glanced out the window again, and a thought popped into her mind from nowhere. *The mountains are still there. You just can't see them.* Was it another platitude? Not exactly. For some reason it sounded like the still, small voice she heard in her heart.

She nodded, assenting to some silent lesson.

"Okay, Lord," she whispered glumly. "You get Jon out. I'll do the Uganda report."

There it was again, on the answering machine. The fuzzy, overseas line. The beeps. The voice, "Elisabeth Casey, this is Badr. I have information for you. Please call me." This time he left a number.

Betty was still at work. As usual, she checked her messages every hour or two "just in case." Now that she'd heard from Lebanon again, should she call Mike Brody? Why not?

Should I wait 'til after work? He'll be gone by then, and I don't want to bother him at home.

She dialed the number in Virginia.

"Brody," he answered sharply on the first ring.

"Mike? This is Betty in California."

"Betty!" Mike's voice warmed immediately. "How nice to hear from you! How are you?"

"I'm okay I guess. How are you doing?"

"Can't complain. What's going on out there in California, or did you just call to cheer me up?"

Betty smiled, wondering if she really was a bright spot in Mike's day. "It's smoggy and I just got another call from that guy in Lebanon. He wants me to phone him."

"Why don't you run the phone number by me . . . just in case."

Sometimes Betty suspected that everything she told Mike was immediately vacuumed into a gargantuan mainframe computer. She desperately wanted to think he was actually doing something with the information she gave him. But some sort of acumen told her Mike was simply a collector of facts for somebody else, not a man of action himself. Nevertheless she continued to talk to him.

"Mike, should I try to get a hold of him?"

"You can try if you want, but don't be too surprised if you don't get through. He'll probably call back anyway."

"Do you think he's trying to help Jon?"

Mike chuckled. "Well, I'd like to think so, Betty. Perhaps he does have a personal concern for Jon. Most likely, though, he's after something for himself."

"Like what?"

"Money. Maybe a green card. He might even be trying to set up some sort of quid pro quo."

"A what?"

"A ransom."

"So you think he's actually in touch with the kidnappers?" Betty was starting to get excited.

"That's not what I said. I said he's after something for himself, whether he's in touch with them or not. And even if he is in touch with them, Betty, it doesn't mean he has the kind of clout to affect Jon's captivity one way or the other."

"Could he get a message to him from me?"

"Maybe, for a fee . . ."

"How much?"

"Betty, wait a minute. You're jumping to conclusions. This man may or may not know the kidnappers. And even if he does know them, he may be nothing more than an old school chum or a distant relative. Everything in Lebanon has a price tag these days. That's especially true when it comes to anything involving the hostages. And, believe me, Betty, you don't always get what you pay for."

"Can I tell him to give Jon my love?"

Mike missed a beat before he answered. "Don't tell him anything until you find out what he wants. Check back with me if you hear from him again. And thanks for calling, Betty. It's good to hear your voice."

She hung up, feeling mildly uplifted. Maybe, just maybe, this Badr person actually had access to Jon. If she could just get a message to him, a word of encouragement. An idea dawned. Maybe she could pay Badr to deliver a letter—maybe she'd even send a poem. Jon would like that.

It's a million-to-one chance, but it's worth the try.

Two days later she had just turned off the eleven o'clock news when the phone rang. As always, she thought it was "the call." Instead, it was Badr, calling from Lebanon again.

"I have information for you about our friend," he told her between the hisses and pops of the long-distance line.

"What kind of information do you have?"

"Forgive me, but I cannot discuss this on the phone. I'm sure you understand. Can you meet me in Europe?"

Betty wanted very much to make a deal with this man, despite Brody's cautious admonitions. "I have no money to go to Europe." She paused, then took the leap. "But I will pay you if you'll do something for me."

"What can I do for you and our friend? I am pleased to try."

"I'm going to send you a letter and a check. Can you cash an American check there?"

"Yes. Of course. How much?"

"I'll send . . ." Betty tried to mentally balance her check-book before answering. What could she spare? Nothing really, but . . .

"I'll send you a hundred dollars."

"This is very kind, Elisabeth. You want me to deliver this letter to our friend, yes?"

"That's right. Are you sure you can get it to him?"

"Of course. Of course. You send it to this address. I take care of everything for you, Elisabeth."

Betty excitedly jotted down everything he told her. She zealously double-checked the spelling of each word. Once they'd hung up, she immediately reached for her stationery and began to write.

> Dear Jon,
>
> I don't know if you'll ever receive this letter or not. I'm sending it with a man who says he knows you and that he'll see that it gets into your hands. I can only hope he's as good as his word.
>
> All is well here, for the most part. All your friends are doing fine, except for their sadness in knowing about your ordeal.
>
> And as for me, Jon, I love you and miss you so terribly. I feel powerless because there's nothing I can do to help you except pray. But please be sure that my prayers are with you constantly, as are those of so many others all over the world. Someone even

gave me a prayer bracelet with your name inscribed
on it. I wear it on my left wrist—it's on the same
hand as the beautiful diamond ring you gave me.

Please be strong and courageous, Jon. Don't be
afraid—God is with you even if you don't feel His
presence. And be completely assured of my love
for you. It is written in my heart.

I'm sending a poem to you. When I wrote it, I
meant to give it to you as a little wedding gift. But
here it is now—in my heart I believe we are already
married.

I love you, Jon, more than ever.

Betty

On a separate sheet she carefully copied the poem. It
was the one she had composed months before while sitting in the shadow of the tower at Victoria Beach.

As, with a cry, I drew first breath,
   This soul began to live,
And Love was lit within my breast—
A feeble wick, of no use to the rest.
Still, burn it did. But why?
It flickered 'til it caught alight.
It warmed my father's face.
And on the men who shared my room
It gleamed and glowed; though futile in the gloom,
Still burned. It had to try.
Then spurning seas and spanning worlds,
You smiled 'til shadows fled;
'Til Love blazed brighter than the sun,
Flashed fire, flared hot, and melded us as one.
Still burn, Love. Never die!

She read and reread the letter folded and unfolded the poem. Would he understand it? Was it too vague or too arty? At last she sealed them into an envelope. She wrote out a check for $100, and sealed it and the first envelope into a second one.

I'm a fool to be doing this. And heaven help me if Brody ever finds out. She had smiled at the thought of doing something behind his back. *Mr. Information.*

She studied the address she'd printed on the carrier envelope, confirming each number and letter. Then, grabbing her purse, she threw a coat on over her nightgown, slipped on some shoes and ran out the front door.

Once she was at the Post Office she realized she had no idea how much postage her letter would require. There was no list of overseas charges to be found. Frantically, she bought $5 worth of stamps out of a machine and stuck every last one of them on the envelope.

That's enough postage to take it around the world three times.

She checked the schedule on the mail drop. The next pick up would be at 5:30 in the morning. Trembling, she slipped the precious letter into the slot and heard it softly thud at the bottom of the chute.

Oh, Lord. Please. Get it to Jon, somehow. I know it's a foolish request, but I've just got to tell him how much I love him. I know there's no way he'll ever receive it.

But God, nothing's impossible for You.

The recording studio was located on Sunset Boulevard in Hollywood. Betty squinted as she searched for the addresses posted on an assortment of nondescript stucco buildings. Finally she spotted the one she was looking for, turned into the lot, and parked the car. She looked around at the rundown area.

This is a weird neighborhood. What have I gotten myself into?

As she approached the front of the building, she encountered a locked door with no outside handle. She rang a bell, waited, and rang it again. She was just beginning to wonder if she'd made a terrible mistake by coming on the wrong day, or maybe by coming at all, when a long-haired youth opened the formidable entrance from the inside.

"Hi, I'm Josh. Are you Elisabeth Casey?"

"Yes, hi. I'm Betty."

"Come with me. The ShakeDown session's in Studio B."

Betty was surprised at the posh interior of the place; it had looked anything but opulent from the outside. Josh led her down a hallway, past a coffee room cluttered with boxes of donuts, and finally to another heavy door. A red light, lettered "In Use," next to the door was unlit. They went inside.

Betty found herself in a soundproof booth, monopolized by an enormous 24-track mixer board and several monolithic speakers. Four swivel chairs and a leather couch faced a wall of thick, double windows. Through the windows Betty could see a much larger room where a group of eight ragged-looking musicians were standing around talking. Three of them were white, the rest black. Behind them was a set up of drums, microphones, and synthesizers. There were two electric guitars and a bass.

An unshaven man seated in the booth looked up and smiled politely.

"This is Betty," Josh said with a sweeping gesture.

"Oh, yeah. Betty. Hi, I'm Dave Demetrius, Brian's brother. This is Jake Arnold, our engineer. Brian's out there with the band. I'm producing the album for Libra Records. You did a nice job on the lyrics. Wait 'til you hear Brian's song—it's awesome." Dave was a fast talker and very much to the point. When he was finished, he fell silent.

Jake, the heavyset engineer, hoisted himself up to adjust some tape on a reel-to-reel machine behind him. He had several earrings in each lobe, all unmatched. "Would you like a cup of coffee?" he asked in a husky voice. "Have a seat on the couch there, and Josh will get you one. What do you want in it?"

"Cream and sugar, thanks." Betty curiously surveyed the studio. It was cluttered with tapes, boxes, clipboards, ashtrays, and other paraphernalia. But it was spotlessly clean and tastefully designed. Someone had invested generously in the place.

Just then Brian Demetrius came into the booth. Brian wore faded jeans, which were ripped at both knees. A brown ponytail cascaded down the back of his faded green t-shirt. He was barefoot. "Elisabeth?"

"Call her Betty," his brother interrupted. "She's cool."

"Yes, call me Betty. It's good to meet you, Brian. I'm dying to hear your song."

"Well it's your song too, you know. What do you hear about your boyfriend?"

"Not much. Just rumors, as usual."

"Yeah, I heard somebody was supposed to be coming out last weekend."

"Somebody's always supposed to be coming out. The problem is, nobody ever does."

Brian shook his head. "Bummer, man."

Just as Josh returned with Betty's coffee and a fat, shiny donut, Dave pushed a button and his voice was broadcast all over the studio. "Okay, we're ready in here. Let's take one pass on tape and see what we've got."

The musicians very leisurely made their way to their instruments. Relaxed and jovial, they tuned up for several minutes while Jake did a final sound check on the mikes. Finally Dave hit the button again. "Okay. This is 'We'll Never Say Good-bye'. Take one. Tape is rolling . . ."

There was a pause. Someone counted out a beat. The band began a song that brought tears to Betty's eyes almost instantly. First a single voice sang a quiet solo. One by one the others joined him. It was just soulful enough not to be saccharine, and it was really, really beautiful. Betty couldn't believe her ears.

Even though she'd thoroughly enjoyed one of their other recordings, Betty had assumed that ShakeDown would somehow desecrate her tender lyrics. She had been bracing herself for the worst since Brian had called two days ago and invited her to the recording session.

But this—this was really breathtaking. The melody had an almost classical sound, and the singers' harmony was complex and rich, like nothing she'd heard before. Brian had been very sensitive to the words she had written, and his composition reflected it.

Dave cut in after the last chord. "It's happening, guys. Sounds good. But the bass is too hot, Phil. Tom, back off a little on the synth until verse two, and then give me a little more reverb. Let's do it again. 'We'll Never Say Goodbye.' Take Two. We're rolling."

As far as Betty was concerned, the song was perfect the first time. The musical subtleties that troubled Dave were completely inaudible to her. Whatever he was striving for was irrelevant as far as she was concerned. The more they played the song, the more she loved it.

I can't wait for Jon to hear this.

Dave asked for three more passes before he was satisfied. Finally he called the band into the booth to listen. Jake turned the speakers up and started the tape. Everyone fell silent, concentrating on the newly birthed tune.

When it was over, the musicians didn't say much. They looked at each with knowing smiles and nods, quietly delighted with their accomplishment. "Yes!" said the drummer, gesturing thumbs up to his friends, unable to restrain his enthusiasm.

"Are you the lady who wrote the words?" the bass player asked Betty.

"Yes, I am. I'm Betty Casey."

Dave jumped in. "Sorry, Betty, I forgot to introduce you. We aren't real formal around here. Guys? Betty Casey. Betty Casey, ShakeDown. Betty, we're going to try and release this tune as a single, and we're looking into international distribution for it. Maybe your man will hear it in Lebanon. Who knows?"

Not knowing what else to say, Betty got up to leave. "It's wonderful. I love it. Brian, you did a super job. I don't know what I was expecting, but it's so much better than I thought it would be."

"Do you want me to send you a couple of cassettes once it's mixed? It won't be on the market for a few weeks, but I'll send you some personal copies this week if you want."

"Yes, please. Thanks guys." She waved to the band in the studio. They were making their way back to the microphones, getting ready to record the next song. Several of them waved back.

Betty smiled at Dave. "I'm really excited about the song."

"So are we. It's a happening tune."

As much as she'd enjoyed the music, Betty was glad to be on her way. She'd never been inside a recording studio before or had any contact with musicians. Theirs was a different world, to be sure. And in some ways they were a strange group. *Nice but bizarre*, she concluded.

Ah, but the song! It haunted Betty—she couldn't get it out of her mind. After several days she found the courage to call Brian and ask him the question she'd been rehearsing for some time.

"Do you think the guys in the band would mind if I played the song at my wedding, once Jon gets out?"

"Of course we don't mind. It's your song, too. Besides all of the guys are feeling bad about you and your boyfriend. We'd like to come to your wedding and celebrate with you!"

"Well, you're certainly invited. I just wish I could give you a confirmed date."

"Yeah, I guess that's a little tough at the moment. By the way Betty, did I tell you we're pretty sure we're going to be getting airplay in the U.K.?"

"No, you didn't. What does that mean, anyway?"

"It means that if we're on BBC, the tune might be broadcast into Lebanon."

"Well, Jon won't know it's for him, but he'll love the song."

"I think he'll know it's for him."

"Why is that?"

"Because we decided to tell him."

"What do you mean? "

"In the final mix, we decided to add something. At the end of the song, I said, real soft, "Hey Jon, it's time you got yourself out of Beirut and came home, man. Your lady's waiting."

Betty hesitated. "It doesn't sound corny, does it?"

Brian laughed. "No, it's cool, don't worry. I'm sending you a demo tomorrow. It's a love letter, man. He'll know."

As it turned out, Brian was right. The final tag line on the recording worked surprisingly well. It gave a personal touch to the song, and if Jon ever did happen to hear it, he'd certainly have something to think about.

If he heard it.

Months had passed since the kidnapping. It was nearly March, and Betty was still alone. Day after day she drove to the office, worked on the Uganda report, checked her phone messages, made small talk with Jim, Joyce, and the others, and drove home again. Her father called every few weeks, but his very evident pessimism about Jon's circumstances only compounded her distress. He'd obviously been talking to Red Jeffrey.

Badr hadn't called for weeks, and Betty hadn't called Mike Brody. Besides the fact that she had no reason to contact him, she was secretly afraid of what he might say. Suppose her letter to Badr had been intercepted? The check had cleared the bank weeks ago, but anyone in Lebanon could have cashed it and she'd have been none the wiser.

The only good news she could think of was that ShakeDown's "We'll Never Say Good-bye" was on the radio now and then. Oddly, whenever Betty heard it, she felt a strange emotional detachment. Like everything else that was related to Jon, the song had taken on a sense of unreality.

Jon was beginning to seem like a figment of Betty's imagination. The diamond on her hand still sparkled in the light. The silver prayer bracelet still curved around her left wrist. Jon's portrait still adorned her room. But Jon himself was fading from her memory. She couldn't quite remember the sound of his voice. She wasn't sure anymore about the shade of his blue eyes. But worst of all she was beginning to wonder about something far more disconcerting.

Was Jon still alive?

From what she'd read, some hostages had vanished and had never resurfaced again. Granted, Jon's picture had appeared on the day of his abduction, but that was the last word anyone had heard. Of course Badr had said, "He's good, very good." However, Betty wasn't at all sure of Badr's credentials as a "reliable source."

A poem, written on the back of a church bulletin, was stuck in Betty's Bible—a Bible that hadn't been opened for days. The poem read,

> Lost
> Between the warm radiance of your welcome
> And the unthinkable blackness of farewell
> I tremble in a half-light:
> Watching
> Waiting
> Wondering.

Betty had tried to find something in the Bible to comfort her heart. She'd read Psalms. And passages about restoration in the Old Testament. And words about faith from the New Testament. But nothing reached her heart. Nothing seemed to permeate the heavy sorrow that clung to her.

One day her friend Erica called from Orange Hills. "Betty, I've had you on my mind. How are you doing?"

"Oh, I'm fine, I guess. I'm still breathing."

"It's been a long time since we've seen you."

"Yeah, I've been sticking pretty close to home."

"I can imagine you would be. But, look, we're having a special prayer service for the Lebanon hostages on Sunday morning. We'd like to invite you to be our guest. After the service, maybe we can all go out to eat and visit."

"Oh, Erica. That's so nice of you. Are other hostage family members coming?"

"No, it's not that kind of a service—nothing public—just our usual morning service, but we want to have special prayers for them—and for you. Can you join us?"

I don't want to drive all the way over there.

"Uh, sure, Erica. That's really kind of you. Did you say it's at eleven?"

Chronic depression had all but immobilized Betty, especially on weekends when she didn't have to be at work. She hadn't been to church in months. In fact, she had no inclination to get out of bed, get dressed, or see anyone. She was becoming increasingly reclusive, sometimes not even talking to her closest friends when they phoned. Betty was sleepy all the time and dozed off several times a day. A peculiar series of aches and pains were also beginning to worry her. The hypochondria she'd overcome as a younger woman had returned with a vengeance.

I'll probably be dead before he gets out.

Thoughts of cancer, obscure muscle diseases, and heart trouble crept into her mind in the darkest hours of the night. Panic gripped her from time to time. She would awaken from a sound sleep sweaty, shaking and nauseous.

Worst of all, she had lost her sense of hope. She had learned too quickly how devastating false hope could be to her. So, little by little, she had rejected all hope. There seemed to be safety in that posture, at least from disappointment. But the gathering darkness was potentially more dangerous than any deferred dreams could ever have been.

She steeled herself this Sunday morning for the trip to Erica's church. There were a thousand reasons not to go, and Betty could have kicked herself for not thinking of one when Erica invited her. In the first place, she had no idea what an Episcopal church service was like. In the second, she didn't want to hear the usual passages about "Waiting on the Lord." She'd heard them all. She'd tried to believe them. She was still waiting.

Just before eleven, she parked in front of a well-tended stone sanctuary, got out of her car, and all but dragged herself inside. The pain that had stabbed through her chest for months gnawed at her again. Erica found her just as she walked through the tall, wooden doors. They embraced. "You've lost weight, Betty." Erica's eyes reflected concern at her friend's haggard appearance. As they found a seat together, Betty noticed that the building was nearly full.

Erica knelt and prayed for a few moments before she sat down on the pew. Somehow Betty wanted to join her, but she didn't. Things were already more different than she'd imagined, and the service hadn't even begun. A guitarist, a flautist, and a keyboard player stood at the front of the church, waiting for something.

Betty started when a voice from the back said, "Would the congregation please rise?"

Everyone stood.

A teenager in a white robe with shoulder-length hair proudly carried a golden cross down the center aisle. He was followed by two white-robed acolytes and three priests. Some of the older people bowed when the cross passed. For some reason, their ritual brought tears to Betty's eyes.

A priest said, "Blessed be God: Father, Son, and Holy Spirit."

The people responded, "And blessed be His kingdom, now and forever. Amen."

With that the music began—beautiful songs of praise and thanksgiving. Some of them were familiar to Betty, others were not. After the music, there were Scripture readings and a brief lesson.

Ken Townsend's sermon had nothing to do with waiting on the Lord. Or victorious faith. Or hostages. Perhaps that's why Betty gave him her full attention. The message was on the Word of the Lord—but Ken was talking about more than reading the Bible.

"The Word of God, spoken to our hearts, is His most vital provision for our walk through life. Why do we go through difficulties? Holy Scripture tells us this:

"'Remember how the Lord your God led you all the way in the desert these forty years, to humble you and to test you in order to know what was in your heart, whether or not you would keep his commands. He humbled you causing you to hunger and then feeding you with manna . . . to teach you that man does not live on bread alone, but on every word that comes from the mouth of the Lord.'

"No matter what we're going through, God speaks to us in our hearts. But we must quiet ourselves to hear Him. Yes, we have His written Word, an objective truth on which all other revelation must agree. But God has words for you alone, about your own journey through the desert. About your own hunger and thirst. About your own needs being met.

"'Be still,' He says to you today, 'and listen to my voice.'"

Betty found herself moved to tears by Ken's teaching. She remembered hearing the voice of God herself. Why had He fallen silent during these last, terrible months? The truth was troubling. Maybe He hadn't been silent at all. Perhaps she had simply refused to listen.

The congregation prayed for all the hostages, and Betty was surprised at their familiarity with the subject. The people seemed to know not only the captives' names, but the names of their family members too. Several people also had a keen political awareness of the hostage dilemma that provided them with specific insight as they prayed.

When the Eucharist began, more tears accompanied Betty to the altar. She remembered sharing communion with Jon, both in church and privately. Would it offend God if she ate and drank for both of them?

Lord, I can only hope Jon is alive. But if he is, I want You to strengthen him with this bread and wine too. There's no way he can take communion where he is. So since we're supposed to be one, please allow me to take it for him.

She took the bread in her cupped hands and put it in her mouth. Although her eyes were closed, when she drank the wine she was warmed by an unanticipated awareness that burst into her mind with blinding rays of hope.

Jon is alive. Of course he's alive. There's no question about it.

After the service, several people asked Betty if they could pray with her. By that time she had no reason to resist.

She knelt in front of the altar and was soon surrounded by eight or ten parishioners, including the Walkers and two other couples from Erica's dinner party. They placed their hands on her and began to pray, very softly so she couldn't hear.

Lord, I'm listening, if You have anything to say.

A man spoke quietly, "I believe the Lord would say this to you,

'You have my Spirit within you,
And my Spirit is grieved with my son Jon's plight.
Just as Jon's love has opened up your heart.
So your love is the key to his deliverance.
Pray for my son.
I know I can trust you to do this.

Bind the strong Man,
Pray unfailingly for him, and I will accomplish his
deliverance
Through your prayers,
Your words,
And your heart of love.
I will deliver my son.
Both of you will hunger and thirst no more.'"

A woman quietly asked, "May I read a Scripture?"
"Please do."
"I'm reading from Psalm 18."

He reached down from on high and took hold of me;
He drew me out of deep waters.
He rescued me from my powerful enemy,

From my foes who were too strong for me.
They confronted me in the day of my disaster,
But the Lord was my support.
He brought me into a spacious place;
He rescued me because he delighted in me."

Betty looked at the people around her. "When that
message said, 'I will accomplish this through your prayers
and your words,' I couldn't help but think of something.
I haven't told anybody this, but . . ."

Feeling foolish but determined, Betty explained about
the letter and the poem she had sent. She also told the
men and women about the song that had been recorded
and about the special words Brian had placed at the end.

"I've heard that song!" one woman exclaimed. "And
I wondered about those words. I love it!"

Ken Townsend was emphatic. "We're going to pray

that Jon gets both messages from you. I believe the Lord wants Jon to hear from you. That's what He seems to be saying."

And so they prayed, spontaneously, one after another.

"Lord, I pray that You will somehow get that letter and poem into Jon's hands."

"Lord, let Jon hear the song and know for sure that Betty wrote it for him."

"Father, enable him to hear from You through these messages that You are caring for Him. That You have a plan for his deliverance. That You haven't forgotten him and neither has Betty."

"I have a sense that Jon feels like Betty may be angry with him or that he's somehow unsure of her love."

"So do I."

"Lord, encourage Jon's heart. Help him realize that he is loved, prayed for, and never forgotten, and that Betty is waiting for him wholeheartedly. Assure him of her faithfulness, Lord."

"Yes, Lord, let him know she's with him and encourage her, too, Father. Don't let her feel that You've forgotten. Answer her prayers, Lord . . ."

As the intercessions continued, half a world away a young Arab nervously pulled a crumpled envelope out of his jacket pocket.

"Shhh . . ." he warned the chained figure lying at his feet as he handed the envelope to him. "Don't say anything or they'll beat me. This came from a friend of mine."

Looking around furtively, the guard retreated from the shadowy room, leaving the man alone with the envelope. Listening for a moment to assure himself that no one else was around, he shoved his blindfold up just enough to see out from under it. He held the envelope up to a shaft of dim light radiating from some unseen bulb.

Betty's handwriting, he thought in amazement. *That's impossible. How on earth?*

Before he read a word, Jon acknowledged to himself that the letter's arrival was a miracle in itself. As quietly as he could, he opened the envelope and strained his eyes to read the hastily written lines.

"Dear Jon, I don't know whether you'll ever receive this letter or not . . .

He read each sentence again and again, trying to remember every word.

". . . Don't be afraid. God is with you even if you don't feel His presence. And be completely assured of my love for you. It is written in my heart."

For the moment he couldn't read the poem; his eyes were swimming and the light was terribly dim. But for the first time in weeks, hope stirred inside him. Hope that Betty would wait. Hope that God really hadn't forgotten him. Hope that there just might be a future after all.

He squinted at the poem, unable to grasp anything more than the last line.

"Still burn, Love. Never die!"

I won't, Betty.

He hid the papers under his mat, praying that no one would find them until he could read the poem and memorize it and the letter. And there in the grim twilight of his captivity, Jon made a grim vow to himself.

I'm not going to die. I'm going to get out of here. And by God, I'm going to live!

6

I feel with the families of the hostages, and I am doing all I can to reach a happy ending,' Sheik Mohammed Hussein Fadlallah, spiritual leader of the Iranian-backed Hezbollah, said in a recent statement.

"'I will exert all my energies in this direction. I have sought to close this file with all the means that I have, and I am still working on exerting pressure to reach a humanitarian solution to the problem,' the Shiite Muslim leader pledged. Hezbollah, or Party of God, is the umbrella organization for pro-Iranian groups believed holding most of the foreign hostages, including seven Americans."

Jim Richards was leaning against the doorway to Betty's office and reading aloud from the morning paper.

"So what does all that mean?" Betty wasn't quite sure why the article, which was hidden somewhere on page 33 of Section A, had made such an impression on Jim.

"Fadlallah is an important man in this situation, Betty. He doesn't want to say so, because that makes him responsible. But if he's talking about humanitarian solutions, then maybe there's something we can do about Jon's situation."

"I still don't get it."

"Suppose we work out some kind of a relief shipment to this Hezbollah faction in Lebanon as a goodwill gesture. Maybe it would speed up the hostages' release. If we could do something significant enough to get Hezbollah's attention, it could take the whole hostage issue out of the political arena and make it a humanitarian cause."

"I thought Hezbollah was just a bunch of terrorists."

"Hezbollah is a faction—a group of people with a political point of view. It's made up of men and women, boys and girls, grandmas and grandpas. Like everybody else in Lebanon, they face a constant threat of violence, and to make matters worse a lot of them live in extreme poverty."

Betty tried to envision a group of nice, everyday struggling people who just happen to kidnap strangers as an avocation. "Maybe we could do something for the Hezbollah children, then. I'm not too sure I want to get involved in feeding a band of thugs."

"Betty, there's more to the story than that. Besides, if Christians don't build bridges of peace, who will?"

She shrugged. "So what do we do?"

"Well, I made a few calls this morning. Apparently there's a crying need all over Beirut for dehydrated milk. And, believe it or not, Hezbollah has a humanitarian foundation of its own—they even operate orphanages."

"How nice of them. What do they do, take care of the orphans left over from their car bombings or something?"

Jim was unamused and a silent reprimand registered on his face. "If we can raise enough money to buy and ship a gift of dry milk to Hezbollah, I think it might pave the way for some releases. We'll make a statement of our own, saying that we agree with Fadlallah—the hostages are a humanitarian issue—and we want to do our part in resolving it."

"I guess hostages for milk is a kinder, gentler deal than hostages for TOW missiles. But wouldn't it be the same as paying ransom?"

"Of course not. It wouldn't be a quid pro quo. It would be a gesture, a statement—nothing more. No guarantees. No strings. Just a bridge of peace."

"So do you want me to help?"

"Well, of course you could help. In fact, I've been thinking that maybe you ought to set the Uganda report aside . . ."

Thank God.

". . . and make some calls for me about this. Here's what we'll need to do."

Betty quickly picked up a pencil and pad. *Anything to get out of writing the Uganda report.*

Jim was thinking out loud. "We need to find some substantial donors, and I've got a few ideas I'll discuss with you. We need to research shipping into Beirut and ensuring that anything we send in there gets into the right hands. And we have to find some means of getting a statement to Fadlallah directly, accompanying the shipment, so he understands very clearly why we sent it."

"This sounds like a lot of work, Jim." Although Betty's depression had waned significantly after the Orange Hills prayer service, a lingering fatigue remained.

Jim was a visionary, and he sometimes didn't realize how hard every one around him struggled to bring his visions into reality. He gave her another mildly disapproving look. "Well, it's worth it to me," he said. "Is it worth it to you?"

"Of course it is, Jim." Betty tried to hide her feelings, but she was aggravated by his words. She knew his big heart was in the right place, but sometimes he acted like no one else was quite as committed as he was.

After Jim left, Betty walked into Joyce Jiminez' office and slumped into a chair without a word. "What's wrong, Betty?"

"Jim has this idea about shipping dry milk into Lebanon . . ."

"I know. He's been talking about it all morning."

"I don't know why, but it just sounds like a lot of work for no real purpose. Maybe I'm just tired . . ."

"No, you're not just tired. You're depressed and confused. But, frankly, I agree with Jim. I think it's about time we tried to do something for Jon around here."

Betty nodded. "I guess the hardest part of the whole hostage mess is wanting so desperately to do something and not being able to do anything. But what are the odds of this milk shipment ever happening? Or of it doing any good?"

"Well, it sort of reminds me of the old story about a guy stranded in a boat on a stormy sea. His philosophy was, 'Pray toward heaven and row toward shore.' Sometimes you have to do more than pray."

Betty shook her head, smiled at Joyce, and went back to her office.

Maybe she'd taken "Be still and know that I am God" too much to heart. Or maybe she just didn't want to get her hopes up again. In any case, she cleared the Uganda materials off her desk, picked up a list of phone numbers from Jim, and started making calls.

By the end of the week, her two best leads for funding were a televangelist in Dallas named Ricky Simms and an ex-hostage named David Jacobsen. Jacobsen had no money of his own to donate, but he was aware of several private donors who might be interested in the project.

Simms had what was described as "big bucks" and seemed to object to his name being associated with a highly visible aid effort.

Meanwhile a cooperative ministry in British Columbia had put Jim in touch with a shipping company in Cyprus. The name of Hezbollah's charitable foundation had been confirmed. And a source of dehydrated whole milk had been located in Switzerland.

As always, everything was easy to put together—except the funding. And that challenge had somehow fallen into Betty's lap.

With every passing day, Betty was beginning to warm to the idea of the shipment. "But I'm not a fund raiser. I'm no good at this," she fretted to Joyce.

"Nobody really likes fund raising," her friend encouraged her. "Just remember, the money's not for you. It's for a very important cause. You really are the best person to do this, Betty. You've got a loved one trapped in Lebanon. People will listen to you."

The flight to Dallas was uneventful, and when Betty checked into the hotel she felt rested enough to walk around and see a little bit of Texas. Unfortunately, there was nothing to see. The hotel was situated on a wide street, across from a pink motel. Flat, nondescript fields stretched out beyond the motel's back fence. There were no shops, no restaurants, and no friends to call.

Disappointed, she returned to her room. After checking her answering machine at home, she turned on the television. Clicking through the channels, she stopped at the sight of a beaming, blond preacher. Sure enough, it was Ricky Simms. And he was talking about hungry children in Africa.

I must have missed the sermon, she reasoned. *I guess this is the fund-raising part of the program.*

Pathetic black children appeared on the screen, one after another. They were emaciated. Covered with flies. Clutching cups of porridge. Reaching out to the camera. These heart-rending segments were often punctuated by Ricky Simms' twangy voice, reminding viewers that "for just $25 a month, you can change the life of one of these precious children. Your gift of $100 can feed four children for thirty days. Don't stop and think, people. Write your check now, while it's on your heart. Do it now!"

More footage followed, this time of an African village. Mud huts and outside cooking fires provided the backdrop for Simms, who held a sweet-faced toddler in his arms—a child with a clubfoot. Simms' charismatic smile was turned, full force, toward the camera. "Have you ever seen a more beautiful face than this one?"

Does he mean his face or the kid's?

After fifteen more minutes of hard-sell fund appeals, Betty saw the broadcast to its conclusion and, with a sigh of relief, switched to CNN.

There was no news about the hostages.

Betty walked around the hotel lobby, bought a news magazine, ate in the coffee shop, browsed in the gift shop, and went back to her room. She was supposed to be picked up at nine the next morning by someone from Ricky Simms Ministries.

She couldn't help but wonder what his ministry people would be like. Would they be like him? The fund-raising program she'd just watched was both exploitative and expensively produced. *At least they've managed to come up with some money. Maybe they'll send a little of it our way.*

Somehow the hours crawled by, and Betty slept at last, dreaming of Jon.

She woke up early the next morning—too early—ordered room service coffee and turned the television on. Once she'd assured herself that there were no hostage developments, she began clicking through the television dial.

Uh-oh. There he is, asking for money again. I guess he doesn't do sermons.

This time Ricky Simms was surrounded by pathetic-looking Yugoslavian children. Although they weren't covered in flies, they were dressed in tattered clothing. And several of them were obviously unhealthy. Ricky Simms himself soon materialized on the screen, with a forceful demand to "write that check now—while it's on your heart."

The camera cut back to a hospital scene. A bald youngster languished in a bed, suffering from a blood disease. Simms prayed soberly for the youngster, holding him by the hand. Once the prayer was over, the camera zoomed in for a well-lit closeup of the now-smiling preacher. He spoke in hushed tones about the tragedy that had "robbed these boys and girls of their childhood." An evocative musical track faded in behind him, making his words all the more gripping. Betty was touched by the broadcast, in spite of her herself.

In a way, she thought, *he's doing a good work. He's making it possible for people to see the needs of children and to help out. Sure, he's manipulative, but if it helps kids, so what.*

An hour later, Betty was surprised when she was picked up in a late-model Mercedes sedan. A perfectly groomed young man greeted her warmly. "Welcome to Texas, Elisabeth. We're so glad you were able to come and see us."

She settled herself in the front seat of the car, noting a cellular phone at the driver's right hand and enjoying the luxury. "Nice car," she couldn't help but comment.

"We want our guests to be comfortable. From what I've heard, you've been through a lot. We're going to take good care of you here in Dallas."

Betty was amazed at the Ricky Simms Ministries' headquarters. The building had obviously been designed by a highly skilled architect, and its interior decorator had been no less professional. It wasn't just lavish, it was elegantly tasteful.

Ricky Simms' honey-blonde secretary welcomed Betty enthusiastically and led her to an inner sanctum that smelled of leather and fresh ground coffee. "Please be comfortable," the woman said with a rich Southern drawl. "You are so welcome."

Betty surveyed her surroundings and mentally contrasted them with OMI's unimpressive offices which seemed quite shabby by comparison. *Well, if I came looking for money, I came to the right place.*

Her meeting with Ricky Simms entailed her informing him about the OMI Milk-for-Lebanon endeavor and his informing her about what he would do to help.

"I'll interview you on camera. We'll devote an entire broadcast to your project, and once our expenses are covered, we'll send you a check. I'll bet we can raise more than half a million dollars for this one. I think we've got some old footage from '82 of the kids in Beirut, and I'll bet our production people can put together a powerful broadcast. We're real happy to help you, Dear. Thanks for giving us the opportunity."

It's nice these things can be done on a handshake in Christian circles, Betty reflected quite ingenuously to herself after the meeting.

After a lavish lunch with several of Simms' assistants, Betty was taken to the television studio, right on the headquarters premises. She was ushered into a well-appointed makeup room.

It's nicer than ABC-TV in Hollywood. Isn't that something!

She walked past several vacant sets on her way to the interview. One of them caught her eye—it had been used on the Yugoslavia appeal she'd seen earlier that day. It was carefully decorated to look like a pastor's study, which Betty had assumed was Simms' actual study.

The set being used for her interview was a cozy looking living room furnished with English antiques and beautifully upholstered chairs. She and Simms were placed on either side of a crackling, artificial fireplace. An oil painting depicting a British manor house hung over the mantle, and two small coat-of-arms prints decorated the wall. Simms had changed his clothes and was wearing a tweed sports coat with an equestrian print tie. He really was a handsome man.

"Now we're just going to have a little chat, Elisabeth, and you just say whatever you want. We'll edit it afterward, so don't be concerned about making mistakes or anything like that." Betty nodded.

With that, several bright lights were turned on, a voice said "Lebanon Children's Relief, number 248, we're rolling," and the interview began. Simms managed to move Betty to tears a number of times, not a particularly challenging feat, by the way. He expertly led her back to the day of the kidnapping. To that first, horrible phone call. To the canceled wedding and the shattered dreams. He seemed to know instinctively how to bring up the most painful elements of the tragedy. Because the cameras were rolling, Betty felt she had to try to talk about them. Fortunately, Simms was kind enough to provide her with tissues.

I should have worn waterproof mascara, Betty chided herself, noticing several black smudges.

Finally, he turned to the camera and said, "Yes, friends, this is a heartbreaking story. But you've only seen part of the picture. There are some children in Lebanon who don't have enough to eat and have no milk to drink. Wouldn't you like to help them and help Elisabeth Casey too? Just take a look at these faces . . ."

"Cut!" barked the director. The interview was over.

"We've tentatively scheduled to air it next week. We'll be in touch, Elisabeth."

As the Mercedes smoothly transported her to the airport, a disturbing thought caught up with her. *Jon's chained up in a hole somewhere, and I'm riding around in a Mercedes with a car phone and leather seats. There's something wrong with this picture.*

By 8:00 P.M. Betty was safely in her own haven, putting away her toiletries and washing the makeup off her face in the bathroom sink. She had checked the answering machine the moment she walked through the door.

There were no messages.

David Jacobsen couldn't have been more compassionate. "I know what my family went through while I was a hostage, and it isn't easy. You've got to believe—in Jon, in yourself, and in God. And you've got to get lots of exercise. Are you jogging or walking?"

"Well, I've logged a lot of miles walking back and forth to the answering machine . . ."

"No, no. That's not good enough." Jacobsen laughed affably. "You've got to move—fast. Get your blood circulating, endorphins flowing. But what about this fundraising business? What are you trying to do?"

Betty explained about Hezbollah. And dry milk. And "bridges of peace." He listened politely. "Well I'm all for helping the people of Beirut. That's what took me over there in the first place. I'm not sure how much good it'll do, but let me give you a name and number to call."

Jacobsen thumbed through an address book. "Okay, here it is. Do you know who Arthur Nichols is?"

"He's one of those super wealthy guys back east, isn't he?"

"Yes, and he's also a philanthropist."

"Oh, that's right. He had something to do with settling Russian Jews in Israel, didn't he?"

"Right. He's invested millions of dollars in humanitarian projects, sometimes to the benefit of the U.S. Government. He's well connected in Washington and knows the score. Why don't you contact his office. He told me once, right after my release, to call him if there was anything he could do for the other hostages."

"He could afford to do anything he wants."

"That's true, but Nichols is very picky about what he does. And he doesn't like his name to be thrown around, so be careful. Tell him I told you to call because of what he said to me. And good luck!"

Betty stared at the phone number for a long time, butterflies running sorties around her insides. *God, I hate this!* She took a deep breath and picked up the phone. She groaned, hung it up, and took a walk around the office, glancing at the clock. It was 10:00 A.M.

There's no point in calling him now. It's lunchtime in New York.

Just then Jim Richards walked past her. "Any luck with Jacobsen?"

"Oh, yes. I've got a call to make."

"To whom?"

"Ever heard of Arthur Nichols?"

"What?" Jim's eyes widened. "You're calling Arthur Nichols?"

"You know, Jim, come to think of it, you're the president of OMI, and you probably should be the one calling. You'd be a lot more likely to . . ."

"Nice try, Betty! I may be president of OMI, but your fiancé's a hostage, and that's what he'll respond to."

Betty closed her eyes, shook her head, and blinked back the tears. "Sometimes that part almost gets forgotten, doesn't it?"

She walked back into her office, picked up the phone, and dialed the New York number.

After several attempts failed to reach him, a secretary finally said, "Mr. Nichols will be with you in a moment."

God, help me, Betty nervously prayed.

"Arthur Nichols here." The voice was smoky, almost grating, with a pronounced East Coast accent.

He sounds like the Godfather.

"Mr. Nichols, my name is Elisabeth Casey. My fiancé is a hostage in Beirut. David Jacobsen suggested I call. "

"Yes. The New Zealander. I've been following the story."

"Yes, that's right. Jon Surrey-Dixon. Mr. Nichols, I work for a humanitarian organization that is trying to put together a large shipment of dry milk to Beirut. We're hoping that by making a humanitarian gesture to the Hezbollah faction, it may pave the way for some positive actions on their part, and . . ."

"You think they'll let some hostages go if you give them milk?"

The whole idea suddenly sounded pretty ridiculous to Betty. Her palms became sweaty.

"Well, not exactly. Recently Sheik Fadlallah has been talking about a humanitarian solution to the hostage crisis, and we felt that a gesture such as this might be a step in the right direction."

"I see. So you want me to underwrite the shipment?"

"Not entirely. There's another potential donor as well," Betty said, not wanting to sound greedy and remembering

Ricky Simms' estimated $500,000 in donations. "But any help you can give us would be appreciated."

"So do you think a cargo ship full of milk would be a significant gesture?"

Betty caught her breath. "Of course it would. It would be wonderful."

Nichols was silent for a moment or two, as if he were mulling over a decision. "I'm going to put you in touch with one of my assistants."

Betty didn't want to let him go without a more substantial promise. "Did you feel you could provide a cargo ship of milk, or were you just estimating an amount?"

Nichols said, "I'll do what I can. My associates and I need to do some research into procuring the milk . . ."

"We've found the milk in Switzerland, and we're in touch with a shipping company in Cyprus. The milk will go to Hezbollah's charitable foundation."

"So you just want a check from me."

"We need funding Mr. Nichols . . ."

"As far as I can see, Miss Casey, I can fund this project. I'll put you in touch with my assistant. His name is Ben Shapiro. Give me your number, and I'll have Ben call you."

Betty hung up the phone and ran to Jim's office. "Jim!" She closed the door so no one could hear. "Arthur Nichols said," she pulled out her pad and read his statement, word for word, "'As far as I can see, I can fund this project.' He mentioned filling a whole cargo ship, Jim! If Ricky Simms comes through with his half a million dollars, too, this will be a bigger shipment than we could possibly have imagined!"

Jim smiled and leaned back in his chair. "Well, good! But let's keep moving forward with the other plans. We still don't know how to get word to Sheik Fadlallah, and we've got to get the milk from Switzerland to Cyprus. Good work, Betty! Maybe you're not such a bad fund raiser after all."

The milk project was taking all of Betty's attention by now. She had officially become the project coordinator, since everyone else was responsible for OMI's normal operations, and that was fine with her. Organizing an international milk shipment was a lot more fun than writing a Ugandan Orphanage Report, especially since her heart was more involved in the outcome of the shipment. And she was finding each success exhilarating, which helped take her mind off her ongoing heartache. Even the smallest victory provided a respite from the otherwise disheartening battle.

About a week after talking to Arthur Nichols, Betty was watching television, absently flipping through all channels, as had become her habit. Suddenly she saw herself on the tube, talking to Ricky Simms. *Good grief, I forgot all about being on his show. Why am I crying?*

She watched the interview with a growing sense of alarm. *I look like a blubbering idiot!* Simms' editors had done a masterful job of cutting out every intelligent word she had spoken, leaving only such things as, "I never dreamed anything like this could happen to me," and "I don't want to live the rest of my life without him."

I'll die if Jon ever sees this.

Of course Ricky Simms had asked her just the right questions to prompt her tearful responses, but those questions were nowhere to be heard. All that remained was a series of sniffing, sobbing sentences coming from an emotional wreck who looked very much like Betty. It appeared, for all the world, that she had parked herself in Ricky Simms' tasteful living room, pulled out a tissue, and begun to pour out her troubles to him uninvited—smudged mascara and all. She was mortified.

Mercifully, Simms' segue to the Lebanese children footage soon removed Betty from the screen. At that point, her phone rang. It was Joyce. "Betty, you poor thing! I've never seen you so upset. Why haven't you let your friends see all that pain?"

"Oh, Joyce, I'm so embarrassed. The interview was nothing like that! Some editor cut out all the questions and answers, all the positive comments—everything. All they left was the emotional part. I can't believe it—I look like a total neurotic!"

"Is your television still on? Look at what he's doing now."

At that moment, the televangelist was imploring listeners to send donations to help the children of Lebanon. He referred to the hostage problems only indirectly. His focus was on "reaching out to the Middle East's innocent victims of man's inhumanity to man."

Joyce was amazed by the tragic footage he was showing, as well as by his unabashed pleas for money. "Boy, what a tear-jerker. He's got to be tugging a few purse strings with that broadcast, Betty."

"Well, he said he expected half a million dollars. But did you notice he didn't mention OMI or the milk project, Joyce?"

"Oh, it's okay. He probably just didn't want to confuse the donors. They're used to giving to him, not to us, so he's just representing us to them."

Betty hung up the phone and turned off the television. She felt extremely foolish, and in a sense violated. The sight of women crying on Christian television was nothing new to her or anyone else, but she'd never aspired to be one of them. Yet there she was, baring her soul to who-knows-how-many million people.

Oh God! This is getting more and more absurd. First I'm in love and planning a wedding. Then Jon is kidnapped. Now I'm cowriting songs, crying on television, passing information to the CIA, and begging for money from billionaires. More and more people are getting involved, but Jon seems farther away than ever.

Something in her silent prayer reminded her of the Scripture her father had read to her at Christmas. Was it Psalm 18 or 118? She thumbed through her Bible.

There it is. Psalm 118.

It was the eighth and ninth verses that she was looking for. She wasn't quite sure why, but the words quieted her unrest and made her growing sense of mistrust just a little less acute.

"It is better to trust in the Lord than to put confidence in man. It is better to trust in the Lord than to put confidence in princes."

Good advice, Lord. I don't have too much trouble trusting you right now. But I'm starting to have my doubts about a few other people I could mention.

The telephone woke Betty at 7:00 A.M. the next morning. It was Mike Brody in Virginia.

"How's my California girl?"

"Oh, I'm fine, Mike. Trying to stay busy. How are you?"

"I'm doing all right too. Look, I wanted to ask you some questions about Jon, if you don't mind."

"Sure. Ask me anything you want."

"Well, this may sound strange, but have you ever heard him say anything about drugs . . . drugs like hashish?"

"What? Why on earth would you ask something like that?"

The question made Betty squirm. That feeling of not knowing a lot about Jon always raised uncomfortable questions in her mind.

"Well, we know that Jon has a half brother in New Zealand . . ."

"A what?"

"A half brother, maybe ten years younger, Darryl Dixon. He says that he thinks Jon was involved with some Middle East drug trafficking in the early eighties."

Betty was speechless. As far as she knew, Jon had never ever experimented with drugs, much less hashish, much less been involved in trafficking it. "Mike, that's absurd! Who is this half brother?"

"Well, he's an ex-con who just got out of jail himself."

"When did he get out?"

"Three days ago. And from what I can tell, he's a chronic liar who likes seeing his name in the paper. He talked to a tabloid newspaper in Wellington. The authorities there passed the information on to us. The only reason I bothered you about it is because of the Badr brothers. Those guys are small-time criminals and have had their fingers in a few drug deals too."

I can't believe I'm hearing this.

"Look, Mike." Betty couldn't hide the edge in her voice. "I've already told you that Jon and I haven't discussed every aspect of our personal histories. But I've never known Jon to use drugs, and I certainly have never known him to sell them."

"And he never mentioned a half brother?"

"Not that I can remember."

"Okay, Betty. I believe you. This was something that we had to follow up on. You know, no stone left unturned

... Sounds like Darryl just wanted to be the celebrity-of-the-week. Since I mentioned the Badr brothers, tell me, have you heard from your postman in Lebanon?"

"Not since I . . . not since the last time he called, Mike."

"Well, I guess you can chalk this call up as another fishing expedition for me, Betty. So since I've got you on the phone anyway, tell me what's happening. What are you doing with yourself?" Mike was his charming self now.

"Oh, I'm working on a special project for OMI . . . We're hoping to put a positive face on the things happening in Lebanon. Maybe show them that Westerners care for them a little more than they think . . ."

Don't tell him about Arthur Nichols.

"Betty, that's wonderful! You must be quite a woman to want to help the Lebanese under such unpleasant personal circumstances. What kind of project is it?"

"Oh, we're trying to ship milk into Lebanon for the children."

"Are you all funding it yourselves?"

Don't tell him about Arthur Nichols.

"No, we're working on some outside funding."

"Any success?"

Betty desperately wanted to drop Arthur Nichols' name to Mike. She wanted to impress him. And she also wanted to let him know that she had managed to squeeze some money out of a billionaire.

"Well, it's looking good. One television ministry in Dallas has promised to work with us and generate a substantial donation, and . . .

Don't tell him.

But Betty couldn't resist. "And Arthur Nichols has promised to help us."

"Nichols?" Mike was cooler than she expected. "Really?"

"Yes. He told me he'd be able to underwrite the entire shipment."

"Who are you sending the milk to . . . the Red Cross?"

"No, it's supposed to be go to the Hezbollah children."

"Oh, so you'll ship it to the Red Crescent in Beirut?"
You're telling him too much.

"No, actually there's a charitable organization associated with Hezbollah. They'll be getting the milk."

"When are you planning to ship it?"

"We hope to ship in ten days." She took a chance. "Why don't you put in a good word for us with the powers that be, Mike?"

"I'll do what I can, Betty. That's quite a project. We could use some good will in Lebanon. Good luck, Betty. I'll be in touch."

As Betty hung up the phone, she thought, *Now maybe he won't think I'm just an airhead from California with a drug-dealing boyfriend.*

She drove to work triumphantly, with an I-guess-I-told-him smirk on her face. She walked to her office and with newfound confidence started calling her overseas contacts, firming up the arrangements for the milk shipment.

I wish Ben Shapiro would call. I need to know when the money's coming from Nichols. She felt stimulated by her ongoing success and rather proud of herself, dropping names like Arthur Nichols around the CIA.

That afternoon Shapiro called.

"Is this Elisabeth Casey?"

"Yes, sir."

"The boss told me to give you a ring."

"Yes?"

"We've been checking out this milk business."

"Yes?"

"The boss doesn't think it's such a good idea."

Betty's heart sank. Her face flushed. "There must be some mistake. I wrote down what he said to me. He said, 'As far as I can see, we can fund this project.'"

"Right. Mr. Nichols said, 'as far as I can see.' That means he was leaving it was up to me to do some investigating. And, frankly, I don't like what I'm finding."

"What don't you like, Mr. Shapiro?"

"First of all, this Overseas Ministries International doesn't have much of a reputation. I couldn't find anyone who's ever heard of them. They've got no track record with anybody."

"It's a small organization, but everyone here is honest, and . . ."

"And another thing, this Hezbollah connection. We've got no one on the ground in Lebanon who can get near them. We've got to be able to verify the arrival of the shipment. Mr. Nichols doesn't put money into things he can't verify, Miss."

"So what's going to happen?"

"I can send you a $5,000 donation for your project. That's the best I can do."

"Could I talk to Mr. Nichols again?"

"Mr. Nichols is unavailable, Miss. He's turned this over to me, and I'm saying $5,000—take it or leave it."

"Well, of course we'll take it. It's just that we were expecting so much more; we've already made arrangements."

"Well, maybe you can find some other funding. It was a pleasure talking to you, Miss. I'll put the check in the mail today. All the best."

Betty dropped the phone. Against her better judgment she had told Mike about the milk project. Six hours later the Arthur Nichols promise had been rescinded. Had Brody betrayed her?

She slowly got to her feet and walked toward Jim's

office, feeling defeated and ashamed. He hung up the phone just as she looked in the door.

"Betty, come in! You're doing such a great job on the milk project! What's happening today? Any more billionaires?"

She sat down and studied his face. "Jim, you're not going to believe this, but Arthur Nichols is sending us $5,000. Period. That's it."

Jim seemed more aggravated than surprised. "I thought he said he would fund the whole thing, Betty."

"He did. That's exactly what he said. But then he turned the project over to some assistant, and he said no."

"Did he say why?"

"Yes. He said they'd never heard of OMI, they didn't have a way to confirm any contact with Hezbollah, and they couldn't verify the arrival and distribution of the milk inside Lebanon. Jim, I'm so sorry. I thought it was all settled."

"What exactly did Nichols say when you talked to him."

Betty looked at her pad again. "He said, 'As far as I can see, we can fund this.'"

"So I guess Shapiro's the hatchet man."

"Either that or somebody changed Nichols' mind."

"Like who?"

Betty had never mentioned Mike Brody to Jim. She hadn't wanted to discuss his role in her life for several reasons—most notably because she enjoyed the secretive aspect of their conversations. "Jim, would the CIA have any reason to stop us from shipping milk to children?"

Jim looked at her completely bewildered. "The CIA? What are you talking about?"

"Jim, there's a guy who calls me from Washington every now and then. He's never really said who he is, except that he works for the government. He's asked me all kind of questions about Jon."

"What kind of things is he asking you?"

"Well, the latest question is whether Jon has ever been involved in drug trafficking."

"What?" Jim lunged forward in his chair. "Jon? That's the most ridiculous thing I've ever heard! I've known Jon for years, and he's as straight as an arrow. Who is this guy?"

"His name is Mike Brody."

"So did you tell him about the milk and Nichols?"

Betty was troubled by the truth on two counts. For one thing, she had told the Nichols story for the sole reason of impressing Mike. But the other reason disturbed her even more. She had clearly heard a warning in her mind—three times—and she had ignored it.

"Jim, I shouldn't have told him. I knew better. But I did it anyway. Do you think he aborted the Nichols deal for some reason?"

Jim turned slowly around in his chair and looked out the window. "Betty, I'm going to tell you something. I think that a lot of people involved in international travel for business are approached by the 'Company' at some time or another. Chances are, we don't even know who we're talking to when it happens. But they're pros—they have a way of finding out what they want to know, whether we mean to tell them or not."

"But why would the CIA want to stymie a humanitarian effort?"

"Maybe it conflicts with some sort of sanctions that the government is quietly enforcing. Maybe there's some other deal in the works that might get compromised. Or maybe they just don't want amateurs getting in the way."

"Yeah, I can still hear O'Ryan saying, 'Leave it to the professionals.' But, on the other hand, maybe Mike didn't say anything to Nichols and it's just a coincidence."

Jim nodded. "My guess is we'll never know. But shake it off, Betty, and be thankful for the $5,000. That's a pretty respectable donation when you think about it."

"It's not much milk, Jim."

"No, it isn't, and you'd better get on the phone and cancel some of the shipment. At least until we hear from Ricky Simms. He's still in the picture isn't he?"

Betty brightened a little. "You're right. I forgot about him. I was so upset with Shapiro's call. I'm sure those guys will come up with something. Ricky Simms said they would himself."

Jim smiled kindly at Betty. "So did Arthur Nichols . . . "

"Oh, don't say that!"

"Betty, you've worked hard on this project. But remember, when it's all said and done, the Lord will take care of it. We've got to leave it in his hands. The way I see it, every $3,000 we raise will send one cargo container of dry milk into Beirut, including shipping. That's a lot of milk they wouldn't have had otherwise."

"But a couple of containers of milk isn't going to impress Fadlallah much, is it?"

"We'll do all we can, and we won't worry about the rest, Betty."

Betty's pride in her fund-raising expertise was badly bruised. "I sure don't want to do anything to hurt OMI, Jim. This could be embarrassing for you. You've done so much for me."

"Betty, OMI doesn't win or lose in this proposition. Nobody knows anything about it, and there's nothing in it for us, anyway. We're just doing it to try and help Jon." Jim stopped a moment and studied Betty's weary face.

"And frankly, Betty, I just want you to know how much we love you too."

Betty's eyes misted. *Just when you thought you couldn't trust anybody . . .*

"Jim, tell me the truth. How much money do you think we'll get from the Simms ministry?"

Jim smiled shrewdly, rubbed his palms together and looked out the window. "What'd he say he'd raise . . . $500,000?"

"Half a million, he said."

"I say we'll be lucky to see $5,000."

"What? $5,000? How can you say that?"

Jim laughed at her horrified expression. "Well, you asked me, didn't you? Maybe I'm wrong. But do me a favor and don't write any $500,000 checks just yet. Okay?"

7

The African sky was boiling with clouds. Distant thunder rumbled. Rain splattered here and there in coin-size drops. And there was Betty with Jon—walking arm-in-arm with him, laughing with him, looking into his eyes. They had found their way from the city streets of Kampala to the outlying villages, where red mud clung to their shoes and chickens scurried out of the way as they passed.

Jon was whispering to Betty, lightheartedly quoting the first line of a favorite sonnet: "Let me not to the marriage of true minds admit impediments . . ."

They both knew Shakespeare's words and were planning to recite them at their wedding. Jon had just taken Betty into his arms, smiling into her eyes, when she awoke.

Where was she? Where was Jon? No, she reasoned dimly; it was thundering in Pasadena and Jon was nowhere to be found. Wishing she'd never awakened, Betty glanced at the clock. It was 2:36 in the morning. She closed her eyes, hoping somehow to recapture the wonderful dream where she'd left it.

No such luck, she grumbled silently, cocooning herself in blankets. *But at least I can remember his face a little better now.* Eve-ry time she dozed off, another clap of thunder awakened her.

After several minutes of unsuccessfully trying to be comfortable, Betty got up, turned on a light, and planted herself in her chair to wait out the storm. She closed her eyes and tried to recapture the exact contours of Jon's face.

His looks had always delighted her. He wasn't the kind of man that women turned to admire, but his features were pleasing and he had a fine web of laugh lines around his eyes that made him appear warm-hearted and approachable. Impulsively, she jumped up and grabbed his picture off the bureau. She studied it, trying to retain the dream image a little longer.

"Jon," she whispered to the picture, "I'm so sorry, but I can hardly remember you."

What was it that had made her love him in the first place? It wasn't really his looks—that had come later. It was something else, something indefinable that had linked them almost instantly. Her mind drifted back to their first meeting in Jim's office. Nothing especially prophetic had been said right then. It was . . .

Let me not to the marriage of true minds admit impediments.

Betty sighed. Was theirs a "marriage of true minds?" It had always seemed so. The more she'd gotten to know Jon, the more she'd loved him. And he had responded to her with great warmth and delight. But now, with him unreachable and untouchable, such age-old questions as "What is love?" and "Why do we love each other?" found their way into her thoughts, followed by deeper concerns.

Did he leave me because deep down inside he didn't want to go through with the wedding? Was he secretly hoping he wouldn't make it back? Why didn't I insist that he stay here? Why didn't I stop him? What a fool I was!

Lightning and thunder punctuated her reverie and scores of troublesome issues remained unanswered. She tried to remember bygone conversations in which Jon had assured her of his commitment, but past words seemed meaningless. She needed to know how he felt right now. Had his imprisonment changed him? Had he thought through the relationship and decided it was too risky to try marriage again? Was he relieved that they were still unwed?

Maybe it wouldn't have worked anyway. The storm seemed to have abated. She got up, pushed open the curtains and surveyed the moon, as it broke through the clouds. *Maybe there's someone else for me, someone better, and God didn't want me to make a mistake.* She glanced at Jon's picture again, trying to remember.

But God seemed to be in it from the beginning.

In their first encounter they had been introduced to each other as writer and photographer, and Jon had asked to see her work. She had been faking her way through her first writing job and had nothing available whatsoever to demonstrate her talent to Jon. Nothing, that is, except for her poetry. Naturally she had assumed he would find it foolish. Fortunately he didn't. Not many weeks later, they had traveled to Uganda and Kenya together on a book assignment, and they were soon bound together inextricably.

Why did they love each other? As she had concluded a thousand times before, the bond was, quite simply, just there. They liked a great deal about each other's personality, physical appeal, intelligence, and spirituality. Betty felt Jon was her better, despite his protests. His accomplishments amazed her. But there was no explanation for their emotional connection. And because Betty could not understand it, nothing assured her that it would survive.

"God, is he the man you want me to marry?" She murmured the prayer and then wished she hadn't. What if God said no? But, on the other hand, what if she married the wrong man and got into another unhappy union?

Her limbs ached with weariness as the never-ending puzzle swirled around inside her. She reached for a devotional book and looked up the day's date. "More than conquerors!" the text began. "Right," she mumbled.

She closed the book, picked up her Bible, and began to thumb through it. *Love. Song of Solomon is about love.* The pages rustled as she turned them. Her eyes were bleary, but part of the ancient poem provided a conclusive end to her ponderings.

> Place me like a seal over your heart,
> Like a seal on your arm;
> For love is as strong as death,
> Its jealousy unyielding as the grave.
> It burns like a blazing fire, like a mighty flame.
> Many waters cannot quench love;
> Rivers cannot wash it away.
> If one were to give all the wealth of his house for love,
>   It would be utterly scorned.

Betty closed the book. So, according to old King Solomon, love could outlast anything. She couldn't help but smile. *He ought to know. He had about two thousand wives.*

She shook her head, wondering again why Jon had left her. Regretting that she had let him go. Lamenting that their dream had come to this. Doubting whether all things really did work together for good. Questioning God's compassion. Picking up a pen, she sighed in resignation, wrote four lines of verse on the back page of her Bible, and returned to bed.

> To sad-eyed Regret
> Faith cannot be wed.
> When one is alive,
> The other is dead.

When she walked into Overseas Ministries, International the next morning Jim was waiting for her, a sly smile on his face. "Come on into my office, Betty. I want to show you something."

She sat down across the desk from him, and Jim handed her a check. It was from Ricky Simms Ministries, in the amount of $3,956.20.

"What's this?"

"Well, the way I read it, I think this is Ricky Simms' $500,000 check."

Betty stared at Jim. "But he said he'd give us everything, after expenses Jim. How many expenses could there have been? I flew to Texas—that's maybe $600, including hotel. They had to produce the program. That's . . ."

"Betty, stop. You can't figure it out mathematically! Ministries do this to each other all the time."

"But it's dishonest!"

"Not to them. Not by the time they've rationalized it and explained it to each other in half a dozen different ways."

"But Jim, there's no way to justify this. You and I both know that Simms has millions of viewers, who always empty their pockets for him! You should see his offices and studios. Believe me—they spare no expense when it comes to their own operation."

Betty's eyes began to burn with angry tears. "He used me," she said quietly.

"Of course he did. But we used him too."

"But he wanted to help."

"He did help. He just didn't come up with quite as much money as he said he would."

"I guess not!" Disappointment and anger gripped Betty. "I've completely failed, Jim. And I feel like I've been betrayed, at least in part by people in Christian work who should know better!"

By now Jim wasn't smiling. "Betty, in a way I've let you down in this. I didn't want to throw cold water on what you were doing, but I really didn't expect much more than we got out of Nichols or Simms."

"Why didn't you tell me?"

"Like I said, I didn't want to throw cold water on your project. I've been around this kind of work for twenty-odd years. And when people promise me things, I just smile, say thank you, and wait to see what happens."

"Well that's fine with guys like Arthur Nichols or the CIA or whatever. But Christians are supposed to keep their word. And what about faith, anyway? I thought God was going to help us."

Betty started to cry and got up to leave.

Jim spoke softly to her. "Betty, sit down. Don't blame God for the weaknesses of people. We aren't supposed to trust people. We're supposed to trust Him."

Harold Fuller's Christmas Psalm echoed in Betty's mind. "It is better to trust in the Lord than to put confidence in man . . ."

Betty looked up at Jim, her eyes red and wet. "So what about the milk for Lebanon?"

"Well, we've got more than $8,000. That's almost three containers, isn't it?"

"That's nothing, Jim."

"It's not 'nothing.' It's the best we could do under the circumstances. And, like I told you before, that's all God requires of anybody. Send a fax overseas and tell them to ship three containers."

"We can't even afford to pay for three, Jim."

"We'll have enough. Just ship it and send a telex to Beirut to advise Fadlallah's people that it's on the way."

Betty went back to her office and sat doodling on a notepad. Despite Jim's words, she was still angry. She wanted to call Brody and Nichols and give both of them a piece of her mind. She felt like sending a scorching letter to Simms.

How could I have been so stupid? What a Pollyanna I am. The longer I live, the more I'm convinced that you can't trust anybody . . .

Betty's cynical monologue was interrupted by a call from Brian Demetrius. She suddenly found a more charitable attitude. "Brian! How nice to hear from you. How have you been?"

"Not bad, Betty. Not bad at all. Hey listen. Didn't you tell me you'd been working on some kind of project to help kids in Lebanon?"

Don't remind me. Betty rested her forehead in her hand. "That's right. We're in the process of shipping some milk into Beirut. Why do you ask?"

"Well, our band's been out on the road, and we had a pretty big turnout in a couple of places. Me and the guys got the idea that we should ask for donations to help out with your project. So after we sang your song about Jon, we asked everybody in the audience to give a dollar for the kids. I've got a check for you."

"You're kidding!"

"No way, man! I wouldn't put you on. I've got almost $10,000 here if you want it."

God must like surprises.

"Are you there, Betty?"

"Yes, I'm here. I just don't know what to say. It's been such a disappointing day, and I was just sitting here thinking nobody cares, and you . . . I can't believe it."

"Well, like I told you a while back, Somebody upstairs has been looking out for our band, and we figure we oughta do something for somebody else. I guess you're the lucky party, Betty."

After a few more attempts to express her gratitude, Betty thoughtfully replaced the receiver and stared at the phone in silence for several minutes. She started to get up, to run into Jim's office, and share the good news with him. But she decided against it.

I don't have a doubt in the world that Brian is putting a check in the mail. But this time, she calmed herself, *I'll wait until I have it in my hot little hand.*

As promised, Brian's check arrived two days later. All told, six containers of milk were shipped, the bills were paid, and the Outreach Ministries, International Lebanon Milk Project was laid to rest, disappointments, surprises and all. No hostages were released, but the goodwill gesture had been made. "American Charity Provides Milk for Beirut Babies," reported several Middle East newspapers.

"We did our best," they all agreed, thanking God and Brian Demetrius that the shipment was even worth reporting. And so it was, with that inglorious accomplishment behind her and without the least enthusiasm, that Betty was soon poring over the Uganda report again. She was

trying valiantly to revive her interest in a different group
of needy boys and girls in another war-torn area.

"You know you're going to have to head out to Africa
fairly soon, Betty," Jim reminded her one day as she
lunched with Joyce Jiminez and him.

She tried to choose her words carefully. "I really hate
to leave with Jon still being held, Jim. What if something
happens while I'm away? How will I ever know?"

Jim and Joyce exchanged glances. They had obviously
discussed this between themselves. "Betty," Joyce said
kindly, "you know you've got to keep moving forward
with your life. God's given you a gift of writing, and you
need to be using it."

Joyce was one of those sweet, guileless people who
never seemed to have her own best interests in mind. But
her words brought a bitter response to Betty's heart. *God
gave me the best gift of all, and then he took it away from me.*

She looked at her two friends. In no way would she
ever have expressed such a thought to them. But she felt
it, nevertheless. God had given Jon to her, or at least that's
what she had believed. She had permitted herself to love
him. Allowed herself to think that they would be together
and that her unhappy past would be transformed into a
joyful future. And then, like some cruel prankster, God
had whisked Jon away and left her with nothing but
doubts and broken dreams.

Why shouldn't she feel bitter?

"I know, Joyce. I've got to get on with my life." She
tried almost successfully to keep the angry edge off her
voice. "But my life isn't all that wonderful right now. The
only thing I have to live for is Jon's release. And I don't
want to be in Africa when it happens."

"Betty," Jim reached across the table and patted her
hand kindly. "Communications are getting better all the

time in Uganda. We'll get word to you. And really, when
you think about it, you'll be closer to him there than you
are here. You're the only person who can do these reports,
you know. That's why we hired you in the first place."

It wasn't a threat, but Betty was quick to realize that
the last thing she needed to lose right now was her job.
She nodded, closed her eyes, and paused. She was out of
arguments. "So when do you want me to go, Jim?"

"I'm figuring on late May. That should give you about
six weeks to get your visas in order and your booster
shots and whatever else you need to do."

Betty was struggling with the sick feeling that Jim and
Joyce had given up on Jon. She knew they'd deny it if
she asked. But somehow, that's how she interpreted their
conversation. *They did their best on the milk shipment.
Nothing came of it. So they just figure it's time to move on.*
She fought off the tears that were trying to gather in her
eyes.

*Maybe they're right. Maybe it's time I woke up and faced
the fact that I may never see Jon alive again.*

As if her thoughts hadn't been gloomy enough already,
the next morning the telephone woke Betty up at 5:00
A.M. The hope that flickered at the sound of the first ring
was quickly extinguished.

"Is this Elisabeth Casey?"

"Yes?

"David Engels here at CNN. Do you have any comment on the death threat to your fiancé?"

Betty caught her breath. "What? What death threat?"

"Haven't you heard?" The reporter's voice sounded
almost disparaging.

"I . . . I was asleep. What's happened?"

"Oh, sorry. You're on the other coast. The story broke

two hours ago, and I didn't realize you might still be asleep."

"Waking me up doesn't matter," Betty nearly spat out the words. "Would you tell me what's happened, please?"

"A picture of your fiancé was released with a note from his captors stating that if the U.S. doesn't change its policy toward Islamic political prisoners and frozen Iranian assets, he will be shot."

Betty tried to control the quaver in her voice. "Did they say how long he has?"

"No, there was no deadline given. And there's some debate about the authenticity of the threat. They're using the same picture as the one that came out when he was first kidnapped."

"So what does that mean?"

"I don't know. It could be that he's already dead so they couldn't come up with a new picture. Do you have any comment, Ms. Casey?"

How can he be so matter-of-fact? Betty tried to find the right words. She had to assume Jon was still alive, at least for the moment. If she said too much, would the captors hear her and make life more miserable for him? If she said nothing would he think she didn't care? *Oh, God. Help me.*

"Ms. Casey? I've got a tape rolling here."

"I . . . I just want to say that I love Jon and that I'm praying for his safety. That's all I can say."

"Anything else?"

"No."

"Thank you. We've got it. We're hoping for the best too, Ms. Casey. Good-bye now."

Betty stood up and blindly headed for the shower. The phone rang again. She hesitated before she answered. What if . . .

"Hello?"

"Ms. Casey? 'Good Morning America' calling from New York. We'd like to do a remote interview with you this morning . . ."

"I'm sorry. I have to go to work. Thank you anyway." She hung the phone up in frustration. Determined to let the machine pick up the next call, she made her way to the shower again. By the time she got out, four more calls had come in. She turned on CNN, and before long the report on the death threat was broadcast. There was Jon, battered and bruised—the same grainy photograph she'd seen before. And there was her own photograph with a voice-over of her shaky, feeble comment.

I sound utterly pathetic. God, I hate this stuff!

The phone continued to ring, and Betty continued to ignore it. She decided to get dressed and go to the office, hoping to avoid the demands of the media. With her mind focused on Jon and his plight, she failed to remember that a throng of reporters would surely be gathered outside her condominium. Obliviously, she charged out the door, only to be stunned by a bank of blazing lights and a thousand questions, all shouted at once.

"How do you feel, Ms. Casey?"

"Any comment?"

"Do you think it's a real threat or a hoax?"

"What can you tell us about the frozen Iranian assets?"

"Anything you'd like to say to the captors?"

"Why do you think they used the same photo as before?"

"Are you confident your boyfriend is still alive?"

Betty froze in her tracks. Panic rose in her chest, swelling her throat, choking her words. She shook her head, breathing deeply. "I'm sorry."

The crowd of reporters fell instantly silent. Only the sound of photographers' motor drives could be heard. "I'm sorry, but I'm terribly upset, and I don't have anything to say. I love Jon. I'm praying for him. That's all I can tell you."

She ran to the garage, tears streaming down her face. Her tires squealed as she pulled out of the driveway into the street.

The OMI office was locked. Betty pulled out her key, unlocked the door, and went in, deadbolting herself inside. She dialed Jim's home number.

"Jim, there's a death threat against Jon, and I'm hiding from reporters here at the office. Could you get over here as soon as possible? I'm kind of upset . . ."

Jim and Joyce were there before seven, and they were both startled when they saw Betty's face. She'd been weeping so violently that her skin was puffy and mottled, and her eyes were swollen half-shut.

Joyce didn't say a word to her beleaguered friend. She simply reached out to her from her wheelchair, took her in her arms, and tried to comfort her by patting her hair and praying softly for her. Jim paced around the building aimlessly, searching for some means of alleviating Betty's grief.

"Betty, what's that guy's name at the CIA?"

"Mike. Mike Brody. Why?"

"I'm calling him. What's his number?"

"He probably won't . . . okay." Betty fumbled with her address book until she located Mike's number.

Jim took it into his office and closed the door.

"I don't think Mike will talk to Jim."

"You never know, Betty. And you're in no condition to talk to him yourself, are you?"

Betty drew a shaky breath. The worst of her crying seemed to have passed, but a sense of loss ached in her chest. She had unofficially declared Jon dead, subconsciously preparing herself for the horrifying call that was sure to ring through at any moment.

"I have a feeling he'll be fine," Joyce said in a soothing voice.

"He's going to die. They're going to kill him." Betty instinctively rejected the faintest trace of hope. She was braced for the inevitable.

"Betty, I don't think it's as bad as you think."

"Don't get my hopes up. Please . . ."

"Betty, why are you giving up so easily. Where's your faith, girl?"

Betty gave Joyce a defiant look, and her answer was sharp. "Faith? Are you kidding? You pray, Joyce. You're obviously much better at praying than I am."

Joyce didn't react, at least not outwardly. She just put her hand on Betty's head and closed her eyes. Before long Jim emerged from his office.

Betty tried to appraise his expression. At first glance, he looked relieved. Betty's curiosity got the best of her. "Well?"

"Well, I got him. He thinks a lot of you, Betty. He said to give you his warmest regards. He didn't want to offer me too much info—you know how those guys are—but he says he figures this death threat is nothing more than a bluff. There's talk out of Damascus that a release may be coming up pretty soon, and the kidnappers may be trying to posture a little before they give somebody up."

Betty studied Jim carefully. Was he trying to mollify her? Was Mike? "A release?" she asked weakly. "I haven't heard anything about a release."

"From what he said, I think Mike's heard that from some source other than the media, Betty. I'll tell you something, I think he stepped out of line a little by telling me anything at all. He seems quite concerned about you."

"Well he should be. He screwed up our milk project."

"Are you sure?"

"Aren't you?"

Jim considered the question for a moment. "I'm not so sure Arthur Nichols ever intended to give you the money in the first place. Maybe he didn't want to say no, so he left the dirty work to his sidekick."

Betty nodded. She wanted to think the best of Mike, but the Nichols incident had eroded her confidence in their peculiar friendship.

"Why do we always want to trust these guys?" she attempted a feeble laugh. "We're always giving them the benefit of the doubt."

Jim chuckled. "Well, look at it this way. If you had to decide between Mike, Arthur Nichols, or Ricky Simms, who would you trust?"

"Sad to say, I'd trust Mike. Or better yet, Brian Demetrius. He looks flakier than all the rest of them put together, but his heart's sure in the right place."

The clouds gradually lifted from Betty's spirit. Unwelcome as hope was, she inhaled it in small doses with every trembling breath she took. She accomplished very little at work that day, while Joyce and Jim fielded the calls of countless journalists who persistently tied up the office lines. By nightfall the crisis seemed to have passed. The phones were quiet. The sidewalk was empty of reporters.

When Betty drove home that night, she scanned the street and courtyard for intruders before she parked the car. To her amazement, the entire answering machine tape was full. She erased it without listening to a single message.

For the first time in months she failed to turn on the television.

Death threats. Release rumors. Interviews with frantic hostage relatives. Commercials. Why bother? Let somebody else ride the roller coaster tonight. I'm going to bed.

By eight-thirty Betty was sitting on the side of her bed, brushing her hair. She chose not to be jarred awake by another unwelcome phone call and planned to connect the answering machine to the kitchen phone and turn down the volume when the phone rang.

"Hello? . . . Oh hi, Daddy."

Harold sounded more than a little tense. "Why didn't you call me back?"

"Did you call earlier?"

"I called three times today."

"I'm sorry, Daddy. The tape was full when I got home, so I erased it without listening to any messages. I assumed they were all from reporters."

"Yeah, okay. So what do you make of these reports, Betty?"

"Well, I'm hearing that it's a bluff—not a real threat."

"Who told you that?"

"A friend in Washington who kind of keeps an eye on things for me."

"State Department?"

Betty laughed. "The State Department? I haven't heard a word out of them since Jon got picked up. They couldn't care less about any of us."

"They're just a bunch of pencil pushers anyway. Okay, Betty. I just wanted to check with you. You all right?"

"Not really. But I'm a lot better than I was this morning."

"Well, we're all praying up here. Your man's gonna get out of there one of these days. Just don't make yourself sick worrying, Betty. 'Fret not yourself because of evil-doers.'"

He must have been reading the Psalms again.

Feeling a little remorseful about her outburst earlier in the day, she began to write in her journal. A rough poem began to take form.

> Sorry for the bitter words
> After all You've done for me;
> Sorry for malignant doubt,
> Cancerous uncertainty.
> Sorry for the midnight fears;
> Did you yet abandon me?
> Sorry for the distance, Lord;
> Come, lay Your gentle hand on me . . .

All at once, Betty was overwhelmed with a longing for the unseen companion who had comforted her so many times before. She fell to her knees at the side of her bed. "God!" she cried out in desperation, "I've got to hear from You! You've got to do something!"

She felt herself teetering on some invisible edge between sanity and madness. She wanted to grab the gates of heaven and rattle them with all her might, screaming and shrieking until she got a response.

"Do something! You've got to do something!" She repeated those frantic words over and over, pounding the mattress with her fists. Eventually the beating of her heart slowed and her heavy breathing stilled. Ever so slowly, peace enfolded her, spilling warmly into the places fear had left.

Her voice was softer when she spoke again. "Lord, I need to hear from you . . ."

Into her mind came the most extraordinary thought. *You will be with Jon again very soon.*

Betty's eyes flooded. Had she imagined that wonderful promise? Was she listening to the voice of some temporary psychosis, or had God answered her cry for help? The thought reemerged.

You will be with Jon again very soon.

"Okay, Lord. I'm going to assume that was Your voice. But You're going to have to do something to help me believe. I need to know that he's alive, Lord."

She wiped her eyes with her nightgown sleeve, wondering if she dared tag on another request.

"And Lord. I'm sorry to ask, but could You somehow, some way let me know that he still loves me? And let him know that I love him too. We've both got to know, Lord. Thank You . . ."

With that, she crawled into bed and fell into an exhausted sleep. When she awoke in the morning she was surprised to see that, in her overwhelming weariness the night before, she'd forgotten to turn out the lights.

Jon was stretched out on a mat, trying to read the Bible his captors had given him. He had been puzzled by the unexplained gesture and finally concluded that it was another divine miracle, not unlike the arrival of Betty's letter and poem.

He'd already read both Testaments cover to cover and had begun his second time through. He was arduously concentrating on Leviticus, on the ancient Hebrew law and the harsh penalties God had instituted for rule breakers.

In the background Jon could hear a radio playing an old Beatles' song on the BBC. "She loves you, yeah, yeah, yeah . . ." Instead of enjoying the nostalgia, Jon found himself confronted by a series of unpleasant memories.

Guilt had been one of Jon's unwelcome companions throughout his captivity. And now, with the many Old

Testament commandments fresh in his mind, past episodes replayed in his memory. Angry words with his mother. Disrespectful encounters with his father. Youthful drinking escapades that took full advantage of young ladies' infatuations. Vitriolic responses to his ex-wife's unpredictable behavior.

Jon was beyond making excuses for himself. He'd been through this accusatory process again and again since his abduction, and even his Christian faith in God's forgiveness couldn't seem to wipe the mental slate clean. He was fairly well convinced that this hostage experience was some sort of overdue cosmic payback.

And he was quite convinced that he deserved every bit of it.

For months he'd thought long and hard about his ill-fated relationship with his ex-wife. Carla had been glamorous and charming when he met her, and he had been intrigued by her enigmatic personality. Although her ever-changing moods puzzled him, he had enjoyed the challenge of trying to make her smile. In those early days, when she was happy, he had been gloriously happy too. Unfortunately, despite their times of bliss, erratic emotional outbursts had begun even before the wedding and had quickly escalated into explosions of broken dishes and bitter accusations.

Sometimes Carla had refused to speak to Jon for days on end. At first he'd tried to draw her out, to apologize, to make things right. But nothing had seemed to reach her. Finally, in his hurt he had simply withdrawn into his work and his own interests. It wasn't many years before the marriage had ended, and by the time it happened they'd both felt relieved—even liberated.

But now, in the damp darkness of his cell, Jon wondered how he could have done things differently. Perhaps something in him was unlovable. She had often said he was selfish and detached. Was he?

He shuddered as he vividly relived the trapped, helpless feeling he'd experienced during that marriage. In all his despair and confusion, maybe he had missed his cues to calm Carla's fears. To quiet her with kindness. To reason with her.

A logical question followed: Would he fail Betty too? Was there an ominous, unresolved self-absorption in his character that had been the real source of his struggles with Carla? Was he really all that different now?

Betty doesn't need any more hurt in her life, he reminded himself. *She's had her share already. What if I'm incapable of being a good husband?*

"Oh God," he prayed under his breath, "I've been through this a thousand times. I've broken all the rules, and now I'm . . ."

Out of nowhere, a thought burst into Jon's consciousness. *There is therefore now no condemnation to those who are in Christ Jesus.*

Jon was suddenly alert, as if another person were in the cell with him. "Lord, what are You saying?"

Again the message came. *There is therefore now no condemnation to those who are in Christ Jesus.*

Jon clearly recalled having read those words in the New Testament somewhere. Was it Romans? He searched the pages of the Bible until he found it. Yes. There it was—Romans 8:1.

Jon pondered the meaning of the message, trying to apply it to his troublesome thoughts. *No condemnation. No condemnation.* Did that mean, perhaps, that there was some other reason for his captivity besides God's judgment? Could there be another purpose other than retribution for his past sins?

Jon closed his eyes, trying to grasp the meaning of the words. As moments passed, logic bridled his wild guilt, and the past seemed less significant.

What's done is done. It's forgiven and forgotten, he finally concluded. *I've got to hang onto that somehow.*

But what about the future? What about Betty?

"Lord, I need Your help. I don't want to marry Betty unless I'm the right man for her. I don't want her to end up like Carla . . ."

She's nothing like Carla emotionally.

Jon weighed the thought. "No, she isn't, but maybe I brought out the worst in Carla. Anyway, Lord, I need to hear from You. Is Betty still waiting for me? If she isn't, then I'll have to let her go anyway. But even if she's there for me, I've got to be sure I'm the man she thinks I am. She's never seen me at my worst, and I'm not so sure she'll still love me once she's had to live with me."

Let me not to the marriage of true minds admit impediments.

Words from the familiar Shakespearian sonnet crept into Jon's mind, nearly convincing him that his dialogue with the Unseen was somewhat less divine than he'd hoped. He tried to remember the rest of the sonnet, but it eluded him. Would he ever recite it at their wedding? Would there ever really be a wedding?

"God, if Betty's waiting for me, let me know. And if she is, tell her I still love her."

As Jon slept fitfully, another tune began to play on the radio. He stirred, and opened his eyes, half aware of the lyrics that floated through the fetid air.

First came the smile, then came the laughter,
Hello, here's my heart. Now we must say good-bye.

He opened his eyes. *Pretty song*, he thought half-heartedly, trying to discern the rest of the words. As the music faded at the end, an American voice suddenly spoke into Jon's drowsiness like a comet blazing across a black sky.

> Hey Jon, it's time you got yourself out of Beirut
> and came home, man. Your lady's waiting.

If Jon could have jumped to his feet he would have. How on earth . . . ? Could Betty have somehow had a hand in the recording of the song? Had she written it? Jon wished he'd listened more carefully. Oh, but the words that mattered had come through loud and clear. God had heard his prayer. Within minutes He had answered.

> . . . Your lady's waiting.

"Okay. Thank You, God. I believe it. I have to believe it or I'm a fool. But what about the rest, God? How am I going to let her know I still love her?"

He could hardly contain his inner excitement. For the moment he was oblivious to his filthy surroundings. To the chaffed skin under the chain. To the smell of the room, the darkness and the solitude. God was with him. God had heard him. God had the future in hand. Sheer amazement kept him awake for hours.

At last he slept. Several hours later he was roughly shaken by a guard who checked his blindfold and abruptly unfastened his chain. "You come with me now, Mr. Jon."

Jon's legs were unsteady, and he nearly fell as he tried to stand up. The guard cruelly yanked his arm behind his back and bent it upward until he cried out in pain. To make matters worse, Jon felt the cold steel of a gun barrel pressed against the back of his head.

"Walk!"

And walk he did. Waves of fear chilled him as he tried to keep his balance. Where was the guard taking him? Was he going to be moved to some other location, or were his captors simply going to kill him? The threat of being summarily executed was not the least bit far-fetched under the circumstances. The miracle of the song he'd heard hours before was forgotten as Jon struggled along.

After several minutes, they seemed to reach a destination. Jon could see light through his blindfold. He was shoved into a chair. His blindfold was jerked off, and a blaze of video lights sent such sharp pains through his eyes that he couldn't keep his eyes open. Words were shouted to him in Arabic. He shook his head and gestured that he didn't understand.

Someone commanded in English, "Look at the camera!"

Obediently he squinted straight ahead.

"Read this to the camera!"

He examined several poorly phrased English sentences that condemned the Bush administration and demanded justice for Islamic prisoners in various locations. Suddenly he remembered his prayer of the night before. Aware that the gun barrel had been removed, Jon took a terrible chance.

"May I ask a question?" he whispered.

The heavily accented voice snapped, "What do you want?"

"After I read the statement, may I send greetings to someone?"

The handful of people in the room murmured to each other in Arabic. "Greetings to who?"

"The woman I'm planning to marry. I want to tell her I love her."

For some mysterious reason, after a round of heated bickering, the man who seemed to be in charge said, "Yes . . . all right. But only a few words!"

Jon read the statement in a monotone, assuming that anyone who knew him would realize he wasn't enthusiastic about its content. The peculiar sentence structure alone could never have come from an American.

When he was finished, he looked up at the camera. He frantically racked his brain for the right words. He couldn't mention the letter, but he wanted Betty to know he'd received it.

"Betty," he finally said, managing only the vestige of a smile, "You've always had a way with words. Like you said in your poem, 'our love still burns.' Keep waiting. I love you."

8

When Betty awoke the morning after the death threat, she was a little surprised to find no messages on her answering machine. She moved the machine back to her bedroom and adjusted the volume so she could hear it. Just as she was going out the door to work, it rang.

"Betty? Mike Brody. How are you?"

"I'm okay, Mike. Yesterday was a pretty bad day, but thanks to your little talk with Jim, I've cheered up a bit."

"I was glad to talk to him, Betty. But to be honest I wondered why you didn't call me yourself."

Betty's secret grudge against Mike didn't seem worth mentioning at the moment. "I didn't want to talk to anybody yesterday, Mike. But I appreciate the fact you talked to Jim. He said that you had heard something about a release?"

"Yeah, in fact that's why I'm calling. Keep this to yourself, Betty. It's probably indiscreet for me to tell you, but I trust your confidentiality, and I want you to know that there are some pretty reliable people predicting an imminent hostage release."

"This isn't just some newspaper report?"

"No. In fact it hasn't even hit the media yet. That's why I'm suggesting that you keep it between us for the time being."

Betty smiled. *Maybe this is a peace offering of some sort.* "What does 'imminent' mean?"

"Well, I suppose it could mean anything from a few days to a couple of months. Just put it in the back of your mind, Betty, and try to go about your business as usual."

"I won't tell anyone, Mike. And thanks for the encouragement."

Betty drove to OMI with a feeling of renewed energy. She attacked the Uganda project head on and found herself making significant progress. The impending trip to Africa still troubled her, but that was weeks away. Today she was comforted both by the promise she'd heard in her heart the night before and by Mike's unexpected call.

More significantly, she was aware of a quiet sense of expectancy. She had prayed, "Lord, let me know if Jon is still alive and that he still loves me." In the midst of all her overwrought emotions, it could be argued that she had put God to the test in a manipulative way. But she could only hope He had understood her despair and would provide some sort of an answer anyway. Always curious about such things, Betty was fascinated with the possibilities of how her answer might come.

Around three o'clock Jim called her to his office. There was a tone of urgency in his voice.

"Betty, I just got a call from my wife. There's a video of Jon being broadcast on all the networks, and . . ."

"A video? Of Jon? You mean he really is alive?"

"That's what Rhoda just told me. You'd better get yourself home, and I think Joyce and I ought to come with you. Your place is probably already swarming with reporters, and you're going to need some help."

A video . . . that's the answer I was waiting for! Betty thought excitedly.

"Jim, I prayed just last night that God would let me know Jon's alive!"

"Well, there's your answer. He's alive enough to be taped."

Joyce and Jim followed Betty home in a separate car, and just as Jim predicted, there was a gathering of news-people outside her condo. Jim took charge immediately. "Ms. Casey hasn't seen the video yet. We're going inside to see it before she makes any comment."

Again Betty was bombarded with questions as she walked through the reporters. Did she hear someone say something about "his message to you" as she darted inside?

They had to wait a few minutes for the top of the news on CNN. Meanwhile the phone rang incessantly, and journalists from all over the country recorded their various appeals for interviews. Betty fidgeted impatiently. Would the commercials never end? At long last the hostage report came on, and the distorted videotape was broadcast.

Jon looked haggard and unkempt. His eyes seemed strained, and his voice lacked any inflection at all as he read the awkwardly written statement his captors had prepared for him. Betty was relieved to see him alive, of course, but somewhat sickened by his wretched appearance. When he finished reading, he looked up, squinting at the camera.

"Betty," he said quite firmly, "you've always had a way with words. Like you said in your poem, 'our love still burns.' Keep waiting. I love you."

Betty leaped to her feet and shouted, "He got my poem! I don't believe it! He got it! There's no other reason he would say that!"

Jim looked at her a little confused. "Your poem? What poem?"

"He got the letter *and* the poem!"

"Betty, what are you talking about?"

"Oh Jim, I never told you, because I was embarrassed and I never thought anything would come of it anyway. But a few months ago a man named Badr called me from Lebanon—some guy who used to know Jon. The guy said he knew the people Jon was 'visiting,' meaning his captors. I mentioned it to Mike, and he figured Badr was probably looking for money."

"I'm sure he was. Why else would he call?"

"Right. Well, I didn't tell Mike, but I figured 'Fine, so give him money.' I took a chance and paid him to deliver a letter and a poem to Jon. I can't believe it, but it sure sounds like it got through to him. The last line of the poem was, 'Still burn, Love. Never die!'"

Jim and Joyce stared at her. "Do you mean to tell me that you sent a check to some stranger in Lebanon and he actually did what you paid him to do?"

Betty gave Jim a sheepish grin. "I sent him $100."

"Are you crazy?" Jim was stunned by her extravagant gamble. Joyce quickly interrupted. "Betty, it had to be God, didn't it?"

"The whole thing was God—letter, videotape, everything. Last night I prayed that I'd know Jon is alive and that he still loves me. I got a direct answer less than twenty-four hours later. Now that's a miracle, no matter how you try to explain it."

Jim motioned toward the door. "That reminds me. What are you going to tell those patient souls waiting out there in your front yard?"

Betty calmed herself. There was no way she could even hint at the meaning of Jon's personal message when she talked to the media. "Good question. I don't want anyone to know about the letter, because it might get somebody in trouble—maybe even Jon. I guess I'll just say I'm glad he's alive, and that I can't wait to see him face to face."

Mike Brody called the following day, and it didn't take Betty long to deduce that he was probing for some details about her contact with Badr. "Interesting comment Jon made about your writing, Betty. Do you think he was referring to anything specific?"

"Yes, of course he was. He was talking about a poem I wrote for him."

"Was it a poem you'd given to him before he was picked up?"

Betty took a deep breath. She was going to have to tell Mike the truth or blatantly lie to him. *Oh, God. What should I say?*

"Mike, you remember when Badr called me the last time?"

"That was several months ago, wasn't it? "

"Right. Well, after you told me he might be looking for money, I decided to risk it. Since he said he knew the people who were holding Jon, I sent him $100 along with a letter and poem and asked him to get them to Jon. Judging by what Jon said, I'm sure he did it."

"Interesting . . ." Mike was quiet for a moment or two, as if he were digesting this new data. Finally he said, "Betty, that delivery may well have cost a lot more than $100. Both Badr and his brother were shot dead last month."

Nausea tightened Betty's throat. *No wonder he hasn't called back.* "Are you sure?"

"I'm positive. It may be that the kidnappers suspected that the brothers were trying to sell information. Or it could be that the Badrs had involved themselves in some other unrelated dispute. They were criminals, that much we can confirm. We'll probably never know exactly what happened."

"Oh, Mike. Do you think it was my fault? I'm so sorry. I never imagined . . ."

"Hey, it was Badr's choice. He took the job. And like I said, he may have been shot for some altogether different reason. Don't worry about it. Just be glad the letter reached Jon. The odds against his ever getting it were outrageous."

Betty felt somewhat relieved. "I really do think it was a miracle, Mike. But it makes me sick that Badr is dead." Mike's voice was gentle. "Don't worry about it, Betty."

"I'll try not to. By the way, is there any more word on releases?"

"Nothing much."

"You know I'm supposed to go overseas myself in a few weeks?"

"Where to?"

"East Africa."

"Nairobi?"

"I'll be passing through there, but I'm actually going to Kampala. I sure hope Jon's free before I leave."

"Well, whether he is or isn't, register yourself with the U.S. Embassy there, and let them know where you're staying. That way you can be located quickly if there's a release."

In the following days Betty was more at peace than she'd been since the kidnapping. Apart from the video-tape, nothing else had changed, and yet it seemed that everything had been transformed by the touch of divine grace.

As usual, after the excitement died down, time began to drag again. The phone was silent. The hostage issue vanished from the newspapers and the television screen.

Betty touched the silvery bracelet on her wrist. Were other people remembering to pray for Jon? It awed her to think that prayers for the hostages were being offered by complete strangers. Praying for the captives in Lebanon had never occurred to her until Jon joined their miserable ranks.

One Saturday afternoon Erica called Betty at home. "How would you feel about speaking to a woman's group at our church?"

"About what, Erica? What do I have to say?"

"Well, our guest speaker has chosen the subject 'God, Our Deliverer' as her topic. She'll be applying it to all kinds of difficult circumstances, but we thought you might like to share a few stories of the way the Lord has helped you during Jon's captivity."

"God, our Deliverer? Is it about demons or something?"

Erica laughed heartily. "I guess the word 'deliverance' has been a little overused in some circles. No, Betty, we're not going to be talking about that at all. All through the Bible God has delivered His people from all sorts of bondage. And Ruth Masters, our speaker, has an excellent presentation about how He's still doing it."

"Is this some sort of brunch or something?" Betty had never felt particularly at home with women's groups.

"It's an afternoon tea."

Oh, yuck. I suppose they'll all be wearing hats.

"Erica, I'm not sure I have anything to say." She wanted to tell Erica that Jon had received the letter, but thought better of it.

"Just think about some of the answered prayers you've had, Betty. I think you've got some wonderful stories to tell, and you really should share them."

Once again Betty agreed to do something simply because she didn't know how to say no. There was only one good reason for going, and that was to thank Erica for her faithful concern. So with that in mind, Betty agreed to be at Orange Hills Episcopal Church on the following Saturday afternoon.

In the meantime, Uganda beckoned. She had pictures taken for her Ugandan and Kenyan visas, refilled a prescription for a malaria preventive and endured a cholera injection. The report itself was coming along nicely. Apart from some finishing touches it lacked only the stories of several children that Betty intended to compile during her visit to Kampala.

She wasn't the least bit excited about the long journey that lay ahead of her but had finally overcome her resistance to it. For weeks she had insistently prayed, "Let Jon get out before I get to Uganda." Now she was beginning to think it would be better if he didn't. Once he was home, she wasn't going to want to leave his side. She certainly wouldn't be inclined to travel to the ends of the earth without him.

Saturday arrived and Betty nervously shoved a handful of scribbled notecards in her purse as she left the house for Erica's tea. "How do I get myself into these things, anyway?" she grumbled as she backed the car out of the driveway.

But when she met Ruth Masters, it occurred to Betty this little outing might not have been such a bad idea after all. Ruth wasn't the typical well-coiffed, expensively dressed women's speaker Betty had expected. She was short, a little overweight, and thoroughly nondescript. But a deep sincerity shone from her eyes. Ruth carried a quiet authority that made Betty want to listen and learn from her.

"Elisabeth, I've seen you on television several times. How are you holding up under all this adversity?" Ruth had penetrating gray eyes, and it was immediately evident that her question wasn't just small talk.

"Oh, I'm doing a lot better than I was, thanks in part to Erica, here." Betty gave her friend a hug.

As their conversation continued, Ruth led Betty to a quiet corner, away from the others, and they sat down together. "What has been the most difficult aspect of your experience?"

"Ruth, I suppose at the beginning it was guilt. There were some things I had to work through. I had to realize God wasn't punishing me by taking Jon away. Lately, it's been fear, I guess. And questions—so many questions. Will our love last? Will we be so changed by the experience that we won't feel the same way about each other? Will he ever get out? Will he survive? Right at the moment, I feel pretty confident about all that. But sometimes, especially at night, everything kind of distorts into a mass of confusion."

Ruth took her hand. "Have you felt the Lord's presence? I know He's grieved with your pain, and I sense that you are very dear to His heart."

Betty was a little embarrassed by Ruth's words, but she nodded. "He's been with me every step of the way. He's answered my prayers for encouragement, sometimes within minutes. He's led me through the guilt, through a lot of the fear, and now it's just come down to a matter of patience." Betty studied her hands for a moment. "There's just one prayer He doesn't seem to answer, and of course that's the one that matters the most. It's become very hard for me to believe the waiting will really be over someday."

Ruth smiled warmly at Betty. "I'm glad you're able to be honest with yourself. And I'm really glad you're going to be sharing your story with these women. There are many kinds of captivity, you know."

Betty was a little puzzled. "What other kinds of captivity are you talking about, Ruth?"

"Well, of course there are the obvious things like alcohol, drugs, and other addictive habits. But people are also held hostage by irreconcilable marriages. By overbearing parents and wayward children. By financial misfortunes. By chronic depression. By loneliness and sickness and guilt and grief."

"So you see Jon's captivity as a sort of real-life parable?"

"Exactly. And as you go through the process of praying and waiting for God to deliver Jon, you can help teach the rest of us how to pray for ourselves and our loved ones."

"I never thought of it that way."

"The world is full of hostages, Betty. Their chains and blindfolds may be invisible, but there are people everywhere who are immobilized and unable to find their way. Their lives are shattered and their hearts are broken. The Lord wants to set them free. And He wants to use our love and prayers to get the job done."

When Ruth got up to speak, she began by reading from Isaiah 61. "These are some of the first words Jesus spoke in His public ministry," she explained to her audience. "And since we are supposed to be doing His work in this world, they apply to every one of us."

The Spirit of the Sovereign Lord is on me,
because the Lord has anointed me
to preach good news to the poor.
He has sent me to bind up the brokenhearted,
to proclaim freedom for the captives
and release from darkness for the prisoners . . .
to bestow on them a crown of beauty instead of
    ashes,
the oil of gladness instead of mourning,
and a garment of praise instead of a spirit of
    despair.
Instead of their shame, my people will receive a
    double portion,
and instead of disgrace, they will rejoice in their
    inheritance;
and so they will inherit a double portion in their
    land,
and everlasting joy will be theirs.

"Betty, Ricky Simms is on the phone. He wants to talk to you."

Betty made a face and mouthed, "About what?" then she reached across Joyce's desk for the receiver.

Joyce shrugged and smiled.

The Texas twang was unmistakable. "Hello there, Elisabeth. We were just talking about you and wondering if you'd like to appear on our broadcast again. We have access to your boyfriend's videotape, and I think we could put together a dynamite interview. Maybe we can raise some more money for your little ministry there. We've got millions of viewers, you know."

Betty rolled her eyes. *I don't believe I'm hearing this.*

"Thank you, Mr. Simms, but I'm afraid I can't possibly

leave here at the moment. I've got to make a trip over-seas in a couple of weeks, and it just wouldn't work,"

"But you're such a pretty girl, and it's a chance for you to be on television again." Simms apparently thought an appeal to her vanity would prevail.

"I'm sorry, it's just impossible."

"Well, what if we sent a crew out your way? We could do a remote interview."

He's starting to sound desperate. I wonder what he's up to. "Mr. Simms, how did you get the videotape, anyway?" *You paid big bucks for it, didn't you?*

She could almost see the sparkling smile on the other end of the phone. "We have our ways. You know we're very well connected with the news agencies, Elisabeth. Would you be willing to do a remote interview?"

"No, sorry. I'm not doing interviews for anybody now."

"How much do you want?"

Good grief. "Look, I don't want anything. I'm just not available for interviews." *Especially with you.*

"It could be a very powerful broadcast, Ms. Casey." Irritation registered in his usually well-controlled voice.

"Well, I'm sure you can find another way to use the videotape. I'm just not available. Sorry. Thanks for think-ing of me anyway." She all but slammed the handset down.

"Joyce, what an operator that man is! Last time, he promised me half a million dollars, made me look like a blubbering idiot on television, and now he has the gall to ask me to come back! I don't believe it!"

Joyce smiled at Betty and shook her head. "Do you really think he was dishonest?"

Betty bristled. "What else would you call it?"

"I don't know, Betty. The Lord said we aren't supposed to judge, so I guess I want to think the best of him."

"The Lord also said we're not supposed to cast our pearls before swine!"

"Betty!" Joyce was appalled.

"Sorry, Joyce. You're a much nicer person than I am, that's all."

Not a week later, Joyce called Betty at home in the evening. "I hate to tell you this, but you've got to turn to Channel 40."

Betty flipped the dial. There was Elisabeth Casey again, sniffling and sobbing on camera. Was Ricky Simms replaying the same broadcast as before? No, worse. This time Jon's pitiful videotape was intercut with Betty's earlier interview footage. It looked for all the world as if Betty were viewing Jon for the very first time while seated in an English sitting room with Ricky Simms.

Before long, the torturous new "interview" was over, and the fund raising began in earnest. "You can help resolve the problems in the Middle East," she heard Simms promise. "Just get out that checkbook of yours right now, while it's on your mind. That's right, find your pen and write 'Ricky Simms Ministries . . .'"

Betty clicked off the television, took a deep breath, and closed her eyes. She called Joyce back. "Can you believe this guy?"

"He certainly has a clever editor, doesn't he?"

Betty was flabbergasted. "Joyce, you drive me nuts. You could find something nice to say about Hitler. I swear you could!"

For lack of anything further to say, they both began laughing dementedly. "Did you write out your check yet, Joyce?"

"No, but I'm thinking about it."

"That's it. I'm hanging up!"

Joyce was still giggling. "I'll see you tomorrow, Betty. Try not to be too angry with me. It's just that Ricky Simms seems like such a nice man."

"Don't they all!"

The time was drawing close for Betty's trip. Two days before her departure, she called Mike Brody at his office. He sounded busy and rather distant.

"Anything new, Mike?"

"Not a thing."

"Well, I just wanted to let you know I'm leaving for Uganda on Wednesday."

"Have a good trip."

"Do you expect anything to happen in the next ten days?"

"Anything can happen, but no, I don't have anything to tell you."

What's his problem? Maybe someone's in the office with him.

"Thanks, Mike."

"Take care."

She hung up thoughtfully. He sounded like a different person and his attitude made her feel a little insecure. One of the reasons she'd resigned herself to the Uganda trip was that she'd been clinging to the idea that Mike would somehow get word to her if anything happened in Lebanon. Now she wasn't so sure. Had she offended him? Or was he just having a bad day?

Men, she sighed. *I'll never understand men.*

Betty continued her preparations with an ear to the news. For once she almost hoped there wouldn't be any. *That's pretty sad,* she told herself, *to hope Jon's release fits into my travel plans.*

On Wednesday, her departure day, the phone started ringing early in the morning. The first call came from a *Boston Globe* reporter. "How do you feel about the latest news of an imminent hostage release?"

"I haven't heard anything about it."

"There are at least two sources for the story this time, and they are saying a hostage will be released in Beirut within seventy-two hours. Any comment?"

"I pray that it's true. That's all I can say."

"Any idea what might be behind this release?"

"I don't know anything about it."

"Any comment about the Bush administration's policy with regard to kidnappers and hostages?"

"No comment."

Betty hung up. Her heart was beating far too fast. She felt dizzy and faint. Despite the steady strengthening of her faith, some symptoms of her hypochondria had recurred in the past few weeks. Would life ever be normal and happy again? She tried to put everything out of her mind except her trip preparations.

Passport. Tickets. Converter plugs. Chloroquine . . .

She took a moment to call her father. "Daddy? Hi. How are you?"

"Freezing to death. I'm trying to keep a fire going."

Betty decided not to inquire about the indoor temperature of Harold Fuller's mobile home. "Well, I'm about to leave for Africa, and wouldn't you know it, there's another hostage-release rumor."

"I wouldn't worry about it if I were you. It's probably just another false alarm."

"But what if it isn't?"

"Well, I guess you'll have to cross that bridge when you get to it."

You're a profound man, Daddy. "Keep me in prayer while I'm gone, will you? I don't want to get sick—that's the last thing I need."

"I pray for you every day. Just relax. You'll make yourself sick if you keep worrying. Read Philippians 4."

"Right. Philippians 4. Look, I'll call you when I get back. Bye, Daddy."

OMI was sending two enormous suitcases to Uganda with Betty, and she had to make sure they got all the way to Entebbe along with her own luggage. Jim helped her check her baggage onto the Pam Am flight to Frankfurt. She would have a six-hour layover there and then fly on to Nairobi. Ten hours later, she would somehow get herself and all the luggage aboard a Kenya Airlines flight to Entebbe. The entire trip, door to door, would be almost thirty hours long.

She shoved her flight bag under the seat, belted herself into the big 747, and settled in for the duration. The flight was delayed almost forty-five minutes, and before long some of the passengers were expressing their annoyance. Not Betty. *I might as well be here as wandering around the Frankfurt airport,* she told herself. *At least I'm comfortable.*

All at once unexpected tears burned in her eyes. With the jetway removed and the plane waiting on the runway, Betty felt completely cut off from Jon. There would be no news, no phone, no word of any kind for nearly two weeks. Was she somehow betraying him by leaving home? Why did a release rumor have to hit the wire services the very day she was leaving?

Her heart began to pound in her ears, but it was quickly drowned out by the roar of the engines. At long last the big aircraft lumbered down the runway and laboriously lifted itself into the sky. The landing gear thudded into place.

Betty was on her way back to Africa.

She sat scribbling in a notebook in the coffee shop at Frankfurt's immense international airport. Betty had hardly slept on the eleven-hour flight, and now she was trying to keep herself awake by writing a poem.

During the course of the journey she had tried to think optimistic thoughts, and had found herself contemplating the joy Jon had brought to her life. True, her times away from him had been marred by insecurity and haunted by ghosts of past rejection. But never before had she experienced such continuing happiness. Perhaps it wouldn't be long before that happiness returned. She smiled as she wrote,

> Hello, Pain—old, familiar—here you are again.
> When I so welcomed Joy to come, to enter in,
> The door was left unlocked, and in you came,
> Bearing your brutal tools, your cruel game
> Of tortured thoughts and fears; and yet I see
> That you have lost some power over me.
> For Joy has brought sweet music, and to my delight
> Love, Laughter, and the Hope of wrongs made right.
> So, though you slash and stab,
> and though I ache and sting,
> I stand erect. And as I bleed I sing!

Yes, it was just the way she felt. Even with all the pain, there was immeasurable joy in knowing someone as wonderful as Jon loved her. For the first time in her life, she felt as if she belonged to someone, belonged *with* someone. Betty copied the verse over one last time, determined that Jon would see it some day. After she wadded up the several rough drafts, she stood up to stretch her legs.

As she lazily glanced around the bustling crowds outside the restaurant, she suddenly caught her breath.

Is that Mike Brody?

Betty squinted across the building. Three well-groomed men in business suits were walking toward the coffee shop in her direction. They were engrossed in conversation, not looking her way at all. The longer she stared, the more convinced she was that the man on the left was, indeed, her friend Mike.

What's he doing here? Did I tell him I was going through Frankfurt on my way to Africa? I can't remember. The men continued walking toward her and finally moved out of sight as they got into the line for food and drinks. Betty tried to decide what to do. Should she make herself scarce before Mike saw her? Would he want her to speak to him or not? He had been very cold to her on the phone Monday morning.

She was far too weary for clever strategizing. In fact, she was almost too weary to move. The three men seated themselves at a table. The two strangers had their backs to her, but Mike was looking right at her.

Spook city.

Seconds later Betty was staring directly into Brody's eyes, and he was doing his utmost to hide his surprise. She shrugged, smiled at him, and got up to leave. He watched her go; his face was a mask of inscrutability.

Hoping to disappear into the terminal area, Betty hurried up the escalator. She stopped briefly in front of the big board that announced arrivals and departures. She wanted to confirm her flight's departure time, but it wasn't posted yet.

All around her, black vinyl lounge chairs cradled

exhausted travelers from every country imaginable. Some of them rested their arms or legs on the finest Gucci luggage. Others had carefully packed their sparse belongings in cardboard boxes bound with twine or rope. The myriad vagabonds seemed to have one thing in common—they were all snoring and wheezing en masse, oblivious to the swarming mob around them.

Mike! Why on earth is Mike in Frankfurt? I'm sure he recognized me—I could see it in his eyes.

Betty decided to walk around some of the airport shops. An electronics store was just ahead of her. *Maybe there's a TV in there—tuned to CNN.*

She was about to go in when she heard Mike's voice. "Betty!"

She spun around. Before she knew what was happening, Mike took her in his arms and embraced her warmly. "I found you!" he laughed. "I thought you'd disappeared forever."

"Mike, what on earth are you doing here? Why didn't you say hello to me in the coffee shop?"

"Betty, I have to talk to you. Come and walk with me for a minute." He casually glanced around, his well-trained eyes scanning the crowded walkways.

I'd forgotten how good looking he is.

"You've got to understand something about me, Betty. I'm not supposed to befriend the people I talk to on the phone. Do you know what I mean?"

"You mean that you're supposed to be detached and professional?"

"That's right. But you aren't exactly a typical contact for me, either." He looked her over admiringly.

Betty dropped her eyes. "Well, you've been a good friend, Mike. You did sound a little tense on Monday, however."

"Our conversations are sometimes monitored, Betty. I took a big chance talking to you and your friend Jim about the death threats a few days ago. You see, I'm supposed to collect information, not give it out." He chuckled a little.

"So did Jim and I get you into trouble?"

"Let's just say I've had the feeling that someone may have been listening."

"Mike, I'm sorry. I wouldn't want you to lose your job over this."

"Not to worry. It's not a matter of losing my job. But that brings me to another point. I'm here because I'm on my way to Weisbaden, which is just a few miles down the road."

Betty's eyes widened. Newly released American hostages were always taken to the U.S. military base at Weisbaden for medical exams and debriefing. "So were you sent here because of the rumors about a hostage release?"

Mike nodded. "We aren't treating them as rumors. We're pretty well convinced they are announcements." She barely found the courage to ask the next question. "Mike, do you think it could be Jon?"

Mike's face wore a grave expression. "We can't be sure, Betty. And I don't want you to change your plans. It could be anyone, really. But I have a feeling Jon's captors may be wanting to get out of the hostage business."

"Why?"

"I've told you enough."

Betty's eyes widened. "Mike, do you realize that I'm going to be out of touch with the whole world for ten days? What if Jon really does get out? He won't know where I am, and he'll think I've abandoned him!"

Mike surveyed the crowd again. "Betty, I've got to go.

My friends are going to be looking all over the place for me if I don't get back. I'm counting on you to keep what I've told you to yourself. Just be sure you let the American Embassy know where you are. When do you arrive in Nairobi?"

"I think we get in at about midnight and leave for Entebbe at 10:00 A.M. Something like that." She rustled around in her bag, futilely searching for an itinerary. "Since it's going to be the middle of the night, I'm not going to leave the airport. I'll be in the transit lounge."

Mike made some notes in his daytimer, nodded and put his arm around her again. "Have a good trip, Betty." He held her firmly against his side for a moment or two. "You're a very special woman, you know." With that, he kissed her on the top of her head, turned on his heel, and stalked off without looking back.

Betty slept most of the way to Nairobi, and when she wasn't sleeping she was trying to assimilate everything that had happened in Frankfurt. She had half considered missing her plane intentionally and checking into the Frankfurt Airport Sheraton, just to see if anything happened. She figured she could always catch the same Pan Am flight the following day. But it would have been extremely difficult for her to get word to the OMI staff inside Uganda. And besides, she'd told Mike where she would be, and he'd given her no way to contact him even if she did decide to stay in Frankfurt.

Mike. Now there was an interesting twist. The last thing she'd ever imagined was Mike Brody kissing her on the head and telling her she was special. *Maybe he wasn't the one who aborted the milk shipment after all. If it weren't for Jon, Mike might be an interesting person to know a little better . . .*

Glancing at her watch, she calculated that twelve hours had already passed since she'd talked to him in Frankfurt.

As the big aircraft touched down in Nairobi, Betty watched the airport lights slip by outside the window. Bittersweet memories of Jon nearly overwhelmed her. Just two years before, they had taken off from Nairobi for London together. She could almost see him sitting next to her, holding her hand. How she longed to be with him—to relive all the wonderful times they'd shared. Would they ever be together again?

Oh, God. Will the waiting ever end? Am I going to spend my whole life in this vacuum? She followed several other passengers into the dreary airport transit lounge. She had just settled herself into a dilapidated chair when a U.S. Marine hustled into the smoke-filled room and began scrutinizing the various passengers who were waiting for connecting flights.

Finally he spoke. "Is there an American passenger here named Elisabeth Casey?" The Marine glanced her way, correctly guessing that she was the woman he'd been dispatched to find.

"I'm Elisabeth Casey," she replied, automatically reaching for her passport. At that very moment, she knew exactly what the young man was about to tell her, and she was absolutely right.

Jon was free! The American Embassy had received word of the release and a request that she should return to Frankfurt as soon as possible.

After all the waiting she was more than grateful for the good news. But she was too exhausted to be elated. She felt only a quiet, intense sense of relief. "Thank you," she said to the Marine again and again. "Thank you for coming to get me."

"We've scheduled you on the next flight to Frankfurt. It leaves in about ten hours. In the meantime, I have orders to take you to the embassy. There are some messages for you there and you can rest."

Thank God I have a Kenyan visa, she congratulated herself as she cleared passport control.

The Marine drove her through darkened streets to the U.S. Embassy, where she was given official State Department word of Jon's release. There was also a cryptic, unsigned message from a German fax number, advising the embassy staff of her whereabouts.

Mike, of course.

The embassy staff couldn't have been kinder to her. Someone booked a room for her at the Nairobi Hilton. Someone else agreed to see that the two huge OMI suitcases were safely delivered to the right people at Entebbe. One embassy official even volunteered to send a fax for her.

Betty debated about calling home, but decided to send a letter instead. She quickly wrote out a message that was immediately faxed to Jim Richards at OMI.

Dear Jim,

I'm afraid the report on the children is going to be delayed for a little while. I've just been intercepted by the State Department at Nairobi Airport. They have officially notified me that Jon is free! Can you believe it? The State Department has agreed to fly me back to Frankfurt, and I'll be going from there to Weisbaden to see him.

Jim, would you do me a favor and call my father at the number I left with you? Let him know what's happened. And please give Joyce a hug for me. I'll soon be able to tell Jon all about your efforts on his behalf and mine. I can never thank you for everything you've done.

Pray for me, Jim. And tell Joyce to pray, too. (Tell her I'm feeling a little nervous about seeing Jon again.) Thanks for everything. We'll all be together soon, and after we've celebrated, I promise to get the Uganda children sorted out for you—posthaste!

Love,
Betty

9

For six months Betty had dreamed of the moment she and Jon would be reunited. She had imagined making lavish preparations for a glamorous reunion. She'd planned to schedule manicures, pedicures, facials—the works. All the fatigue, all the circles under her eyes, all the stress lines around her mouth would cosmetically vanish. She would wear new clothes, new shoes, maybe even carry a new handbag and buy new earrings for the occasion.

Now here she was, dressed in the best of her wash-and-wear "Africa wardrobe," a three-year-old Banana Republic dress and a pair of tan espadrilles. She had slept only briefly during the past forty-eight hours, and then she'd barely slept. Her ankles were swollen from flying, an unflattering condition that vaguely reminded her of elephants' feet.

Worse yet, all the makeup in the world couldn't disguise the weariness on Betty's face. She pulled out a mirror and proceeded to pile more mascara on her eyelashes, more circle cream under her eyes, and more lip gloss on her mouth. As far as she was concerned, it was to no avail.

The Lufthansa flight attendant smiled when she saw Betty re-primping. "You look lovely," she said.

Are you nuts? I look disgusting.

"Oh, thanks." She glumly clicked her compact shut and brushed her hair—again.

What would happen when she got to Frankfurt? Was Jon already at Weisbaden or would she be there for his arrival? When and where would they actually meet? Courteous as the American Embassy staff had been at Nairobi, they hadn't provided her with much information.

The diamond on her left hand caught her attention. She had seriously considered not wearing it to Africa. It was a large, impressive gem and she feared it might be stolen. Now she thanked God and her own sentimental nature that she hadn't left it behind. Jon would have been devastated if she'd appeared at Weisbaden without her engagement ring.

She dozed for only a few moments at a time, always waking with the same quiet thought—*it's over!* Gradually questions began to arise. She became curious about the circumstances surrounding Jon's release. Several hostages had been held far longer than he, and they still remained captive. Why had Jon been taken and released so quickly? Why only six months?

She reflected on the conversation she'd had with Mike Brody in Frankfurt. Hadn't he said something about Jon's captors wanting to get out of the hostage business? The explosion of Irangate a few years before had cast grave shadows across all kinds of negotiations. Since November 1986, there was little evidence of any effort being made on behalf of the Lebanon hostages. Only State Department lip service was paid to "doing all we can."

So why was Jon free? Betty believed in prayer. And although thousands of people were praying for the other hostages, many of those who personally knew Jon were almost fanatically serious about their intercessory prayer for him. Had that been a factor in his sudden freedom? In actual fact, Jon's release really did seem like a miracle. Betty couldn't wait to learn more about it.

When the Lufthansa plane finally landed in Frankfurt Betty took one last glimpse in her mirror, hoping the flight attendant wouldn't notice. It was one of those beauty inspections that made her wish she hadn't bothered to look in the first place.

It's too late now . . .

She shoved the compact in her purse, unfastened her seat belt, and headed for the airplane exit.

Of course she should have realized that the press would be waiting for her in full force, but she had mistakenly assumed that they had all been left behind in Southern California. She was thoroughly unprepared when she walked into the blazing white lights and the tangle of microphones. "We were expecting a big smile," one reporter shouted. "Where's that beautiful smile?"

"How do you feel?"

"Have you spoken with Jon?"

"Who negotiated Jon's release?"

"Did the U.S. government deal with Iran for his release?"

"Are you aware of any secret deals with the Israelis?"

Betty forced a grin. Not that she wasn't happy about Jon's release. Of course she was. But there was only one person she wanted to talk to right then, and he wasn't in that particular crowd.

"I'll see you after I talk to Jon," she said with a wave, "at Weisbaden."

She was rescued by a contingent of sober-faced military personnel, who rapidly escorted her out of the airport and into a waiting car. Once her baggage was retrieved, they were on their way. Betty tried to interrogate her companions about Jon, but they weren't communicative.

"Have you seen my fiancé yet?"

"No, ma'am." The fuzzy-cheeked soldier-driver stared straight ahead, clearly uncomfortable with his role as part of her reception committee. She turned to the other men in the backseat.

"Is he here yet? In Weisbaden?"

"Yes, ma'am. He arrived last night."

"How is he?"

"We haven't seen him either, ma'am."

Don't call me 'ma'am' again or I'll scream.

"Do you know where I'll be staying?"

"The families usually stay in a residential complex adjacent to the hospital, ma'am. But you're not his wife yet, are you?"

"No, we're not married yet."

"Well then I don't know. It's usually just immediate families that stay there. Otherwise you'll be in a hotel in town. The State Department takes care of all that."

Wonderful. I'll probably end up in a sleeping bag on the lawn.

Once her fact-finding mission proved unsuccessful, Betty fell silent, left to pass the time by reorganizing her various anxieties. She wondered if Mike Brody was still around. Why wouldn't he be? She deduced that Mike was probably part of Jon's debriefing team. If Jon had arrived just the night before, the spooks weren't finished with him yet.

Tired as she was, faint excitement rippled inside her. Jon! She was on her way to see Jon! How would he look? How would he act? Where would their first meeting take place? What would they say to each other? It was almost six in the evening in Germany. Would she see him that night or the next morning?

At last the car entered a nondescript military complex. She was delivered to a small building where she was greeted by a State Department representative.

"Ms. Casey? Marion Albert. You'll be staying here during your visit to Weisbaden. Although you and Mr. Surrey-Dixon aren't yet married, we have been advised that you are the only person coming to meet him, so we'll be happy to accommodate you here."

Thanks, God. No sleeping bag.

"Thank you. I appreciate that."

"If you'll follow me, I'll show you to your room. You may want to freshen up a bit before going over to the hospital. If you'll meet me in the reception area in a half-hour, I'll take you over to see Jon."

"Have you seen him?"

"No, I haven't seen him myself, but I understand he's in good health and good spirits. Now if you'll excuse me . . ."

"Of course. Thanks again for the accommodations. I appreciate the thoughtfulness."

Marion Albert smiled. "Our pleasure," she nodded politely. "I'll see you in half an hour."

Once she left, Betty looked around the room and noticed a balcony. She stepped outside into the cool evening air and looked directly into the windows of the big U.S. Army hospital.

Jon's in there! She stood transfixed by the building across the way. Her heart sped up. *Jon's actually in there!*

Impulsively she waved, just in case he might be watching. Then, feeling suddenly foolish, she retreated into her room, drew the curtains, and began to brush her hair.

A short time later, Betty gave a cheerful thumbs-up to a crowd of reporters as she was led through the guarded gate that separated her accommodations from the hospital itself. She exchanged pleasantries with the military staff in the lobby. She was still trying to figure out what to say to Jon as she was escorted up an elevator and to the door of a room. A thin, blue-eyed man sat waiting inside.

He stood up, a faint smile on his lips. "I've been looking forward to this for a long time, Betty." Jon's voice was almost monotone.

"Me too."

Their embrace lasted a long time but was strangely unimpassioned. Betty looked into Jon's eyes. What was so different about him? He seemed cool and distant.

"Jon, are you all right?"

"I'm . . . I'm fine, Betty. Just a little overwhelmed, you know. You look wonderful, as always."

Again she searched his eyes. Dim and dull.

Horrible thoughts chilled her. Had he suffered some sort of emotional or mental damage in his captivity? Or was he trying to send her a message of disinterest?

They sat down and began a peculiar, one-sided conversation. Betty knew she was talking too much, too fast, trying to make up for the quiet, unemotional responses she was receiving from her friend, her fiancé. She chattered, then fell silent, then chattered again.

Oh, God, help me.

"Have you had dinner?" Jon asked. "I think they said you could eat here with me."

Betty couldn't have eaten a bite if her life had depended upon it. But she didn't want to leave, either, at least not quite yet.

A meal was produced, which Jon devoured quickly. *That's the most enthusiasm he's shown since I got here.* She picked at the chicken and vegetables in front of her. It was as uninspiring as the ongoing dialogue.

Once he'd finished eating, Jon began to yawn almost compulsively. Betty searched her soul for a subject that would galvanize him. She had carefully collected countless episodes and experiences to share with him while they were apart. Now his detached, unresponsive behavior paralyzed her. She couldn't think of another thing to say.

"Jon, you're so tired. And really, so am I. I think we'll both feel better after a good night's sleep."

They were sitting side by side. He looked at her a little sadly, reached over, and touched her face with his hand.

Hope stirred inside her. Tears stung her eyes. She studied his face. Were there tears in his eyes too?

"Jon, I love you."

He nodded mutely and touched her face once more. Again, the stirring.

"I'll see you tomorrow, Betty. Get a good sleep—you look exhausted."

Feeling dismissed, she got up to go, fighting back the tears.

He didn't even say "I love you, too."

She quickly kissed him good-bye, rushed out the door, down the elevator, and with the help of a friendly soldier, found her way back toward her residence.

Fenced out, she told herself as she walked through the guarded gate. *I'm fenced out in more ways than one.*

She stretched out on her bed, too weary to think, too frightened to sleep. Fear and fatigue quickly distorted her disappointing encounter with Jon into a hopeless catastrophe. Unsatisfying reality was transformed into irrevocable finality. Irrational as it was, she felt their relationship was lost forever.

If there had been a phone in the room, she might have called Jim. Or Joyce. Or maybe even her father. But why call, even if she could? There was nothing to report except sorrow and humiliation. Betty felt like grabbing her belongings, hitching a ride back to the Frankfurt airport, and disappearing somewhere in Africa—forever. She was mulling over that frantic possibility when she heard a knock at the door. She opened it and was handed a note.

Hi Betty,

Welcome to Weisbaden. I hear Jon's resting tonight. Do you want to get together for a drink? I'll pick you up in a half-hour.

Mike

Fine with me. At least somebody wants to talk to me.

Mike greeted her with open arms, giving her a quick peck on the lips this time instead of a kiss on the head. She felt like crying in his arms but managed to pull herself away and restore her composure.

"Let's go over to the Intercontinental in Frankfurt. They have a nice bar and I feel like getting out of here for awhile. How 'bout you?"

Betty nodded. As they made the twenty-minute drive back to Frankfurt, she was in no mood for mincing words. "Mike, is there something wrong with Jon?"

"Jon seems to be in reasonably good health, Betty."

"He doesn't seem reasonably healthy to me. He's just not right . . . he's not himself at all."

"Well, maybe it's the shock of freedom. Clearly being released from captivity is a stressful experience. But you'd be far more qualified to judge his behavior than anyone else. You certainly know him better than I do."

Mike's words were little comfort. In fact they made Betty feel worse than ever. As far as she was concerned, Jon was either permanently mentally impaired or he was trying to get rid of her. She glanced at Mike. A gentle smile played around his mouth. What was he thinking?

Somehow, they managed to talk about other matters besides Jon's mental condition. They discussed her flight to Nairobi, the marine who had intercepted her in the transit lounge there, the flight back to Frankfurt, the nice folks at the American Embassy. Mike casually deflected questions about himself, focusing his attention on her. Once they settled into the hotel bar, Betty sipped on a glass of Chablis while he downed two Vodka Stingers.

Epilog Bar, Betty noticed the establishment's logo. *How appropriate.*

Betty was flattered by Mike's attention. He was growing more affectionate by the minute. His eyes never left her face, and he was increasingly jovial and amusing. What did he have in mind, anyway?

Oh, God. I'm so vulnerable.

Her engagement ring danced with color as it caught the light around it. Perhaps she would soon be taking it off, giving it back to Jon and saying, "Good-bye. I'm sorry. See you later."

Meanwhile, Mike was asking about her work. Her home in California. Her car. Her future plans. Jon's name never entered the conversation. At last they fell silent.

Betty was staring at her hands, sadly aware of the twinkling diamond that seemed to have come to life in the Epilog Bar.

Mike caressed the back of her neck for a moment, then gently pulled her close to him. Betty was fully aware of the move he was making, feeling his warm breath on her face. Rather comfortable in his embrace, she didn't move. But, just as she should have succumbed to the comfort she craved, her mind began drifting away from her companion. Away from the tinkling of ice-against-glass. Away from Frankfurt altogether. Memories came to her like snapshots in an album, its pages turning unhurriedly.

She saw Jon's first letter, written to her on blue airmail paper. In his characteristic scrawl it said that he loved her poetry and how much he looked forward to meeting her. She was still amazed by his warm response to her collection of poems.

She saw Jon the first day they met, sitting across from her in Jim's office. She'd liked him immediately. Not long afterward, Joyce Jimenez had told her that he had been more than impressed with her too. How extraordinary it had seemed that they would soon be working on a book together.

She saw Jon kissing her in a Uganda thunderstorm. She could almost smell the wet earth and feel the lukewarm raindrops against her skin. As fervently as she'd resisted it, something had captured her heart there in East Africa—-something unexplainable and inevitable.

She saw Jon in the Kenyan night, his clear, intelligent eyes reflecting his love for her, his hands breaking bread for her, pouring wine for her. It had been the conclusion of an unforgettable trip together and had seemed like the beginning of a life journey.

And, finally, she saw Jon lying next to her in her bed. His hair was tousled, his face childlike in sleep. She had traced her fingers across his eyes and lips. They had shared just one night together, and she had never completely forgotten the sweet sense of belonging.

You've got to be patient just a little longer. Give him time! You can't give up now . . .

Betty felt Mike's hand burning against her shoulder, his face against her hair. She liked Mike. She didn't want to hurt him. But she quietly said, "I think I'd better get back to Weisbaden now." And, as she reached for her handbag, she deliberately pulled away from his embrace.

The spell was broken.

Their drive back was pleasant enough, but not marked by animated conversation as before. Mike wasn't particularly talkative, and Betty didn't know what to say to him. It was virtually impossible to talk about his work, and he was unwilling to say much at all on a personal level. She hated to bring up his past—most likely that was another minefield. Meanwhile, Betty had told him all she intended to about herself.

He embraced her firmly when they parted at her quarters in Weisbaden. "Will I see you again?" he asked with a hopeful grin.

"I don't know what's going on," she shrugged, unable to look him in the eye. "I've got to spend most of tomorrow with Jon. But thanks for getting me out of here—I enjoyed talking to you, Mike."

He hugged her again, and she escaped inside the building without another word. She didn't notice the woman who was seated at the reception desk. It was nearly midnight.

"Ms. Casey? You have several messages."

"For me? Are you sure?"

Betty unfolded a handful of small notes, most of them from various media contacts. She sighed wearily, knowing they wanted "exclusive" interviews with the newly released hostage.

Then, among the other memos, she realized that there had been two phone calls from Jon Surrey-Dixon himself.

The first message had come at 9:15. It said, "Sorry I missed you. I'll call back later."

The second message, at 10:50 read, "Where are you anyway? I'm going back to bed. Please join me tomorrow for breakfast. I love you."

"Jon, I'm sorry I missed your calls last night!" Betty could feel his heart beating against her chest.

He held her out at arm's-length and eyed her suspiciously. "Where on earth did you go? I thought you'd decided I was such a bore that you'd run off with somebody else!"

No, not a bore. Just brain-dead.

Betty gestured flippantly. "Oh, I ran into one of the men who's been working on your case, and he invited me to have a drink with him. You were so tired, I thought you'd sleep all night. Otherwise I wouldn't have gone."

Jon was much more himself this morning. He still seemed a bit fuzzy in his perceptions, but nothing like the night before. He stared at her quizzically, a somewhat hurt look on his face. "Betty, I can't blame you for giving up on me last night, but I must say that seems a little odd to think you'd go out with another man."

Uneasiness stirred inside her. Almost able to feel Mike's arm around her and his breath on her face, she shivered involuntarily. "Believe me, it was no big deal, Jon. I thought you were zonked out for the night, and I just didn't want to sit in my room."

Jon studied her face. "Who is he?"

"He's one of the men who's been debriefing you, at least I think he is."

"Which one?"

"His name's Mike."

"Mike . . . ," Jon frowned and looked at the floor.

Dear God, I hope Mike hasn't said anything strange to him.

"Jon, you're making too big of a deal out of this." Betty was trying very hard not to sound defensive, and perhaps even more importantly, not to give Jon any indication of Mike's interest in her. After all, she wasn't interested in Mike, so what difference did it make anyway? Finally, making a valiant attempt to steer the conversation elsewhere, Betty took a breath and asked, "Speaking of suspicious behavior, Jon, why were you so silent last night? I was beginning to wonder what *you've* been up to!"

Jon silently surveyed Betty's face, unable to shake off a troubling sense of skepticism. Finally he shrugged and answered quietly, "I was exhausted, but I guess I was nervous too. No matter how much I wanted to spend the night talking to you, for some reason I was tongue-tied. I couldn't think of a single thing to say."

"Neither could I."

Jon chuckled. "Well, that's a first."

Betty frowned at him and shook her head. "Men always think women talk too much. But you're not going to get away with that today, because I want you to tell me how you got out of captivity. How much do you know? I've been so curious."

"Well, which story do you want to hear?"

"What do you mean?"

"I mean two things happened at the same time. One had to do with my captors' miserable performance as hostage takers. The other one was my own spiritual release, which happened before they actually let me go."

"Let's start with the miserable hostage takers." Betty again recalled Mike's comment about their "getting out of the hostage business."

"Right. Well as I understand it, the men who took me were part of a loosely knit crime ring. They had no political aspirations at all but thought they might be able to scare up some American dollars in ransom if they picked up a hostage."

"So they weren't the same people that kidnapped Anderson and Waite and all the others?"

"No. They tried to use the same Islamic rhetoric in their messages, but in actual fact the other kidnappers were appalled by their actions. I guess they felt it was a cheap shot, since they were representing the true Islamic revolutionary cause."

"Who told you all this?"

"Well, that was one of the problems. Some of the guards they'd hired to take care of me were really pretty decent guys, and before long they were giving me all the inside scoop on my captors. Apparently there were all kinds of spies in the camp selling stories. Somebody even brought me your letter."

"Do you remember a man named Abdul Badr?"

Jon stared at her in amazement. "Abdul Badr? Sure I do. I met him and his brother in '82 during the war. How do you know about him?"

"Well, he's the one who got the letter to you. I first heard about him from Vince Angelo, who said you were hoping to find him while you were there."

"How on earth did you get in touch with him?"

"I didn't. He got in touch with me. As you'll soon find out, this whole mess has made celebrities out of us both—my name was all over the place in news reports, and the major news services gave my phone number out to anybody who asked."

"So we're famous?" Jon laughed. "Perfect. Just in time for our honeymoon. But what about Badr?"

"Badr's dead. He was killed not long after the letter got to you, or so I gather. I've been getting a little information from a guy in Washington D.C. who talks more than he's supposed to."

"Badr's dead?" Jon's face paled.

"Yes. And his brother too. And at one point the guys working on your case thought you were involved with them in some kind of drug dealing. To make matters worse a man claiming to be your half brother in New Zealand was spreading stories about you in the world press."

Jon looked foggier than ever. "Betty, I don't have a half brother in New Zealand. I don't have any brothers or sisters anywhere."

"All I know is that a newly released convict with the last name of Dixon said that you were his half brother and that you had been involved with drug dealing in Lebanon. He apparently sold his story to some tabloid in Wellington. The man who told me about all this said Dixon is a known pathological liar. I guess they listened to him anyway."

Jon sighed and shook his head. "This is unbelievable. I had no idea rats like that would crawl out of the woodwork. I guess saying he was my brother seemed like a fast way to make a buck."

"There's more money in the hostage issue than you might imagine, Jon," Betty remarked, choosing to save her Ricky Simms saga for some future conversation.

"Just for the record, I met the Badr brothers on my first trip to Lebanon, and I'm pretty sure they were small-time criminals. For all I know they may have been involved in hashish—a lot of people are. But they were likable guys and seemed to know everybody in the country. I had befriended them by taking pictures of their family for an anniversary or birthday or something—I don't remember. Anyway, I figured they might help Vince and me out on our assignment. So you say Abdul got the letter to me?"

"Yeah, for $100." Betty looked at Jon sheepishly.

Jon laughed in spite of himself. "It was worth it, believe me." He put his arm around her and kissed her on the cheek. "That was quite a poem. In any case, my guards were letting me know that the men holding me were getting no ransom offers, and my care was costing them more than they expected. At one point they were going to shoot me, but God took care of that."

"What did God do?"

"One of the guards brought his son to work with him sometimes, if you can believe it. The little guy was about four or five and he had a pretty bad rash on his arms and legs. I had the strongest feeling I should pray for him—I guess I remembered your skin problem, and I asked the boy's father if he'd mind. Of course he couldn't have cared less. I put my hand on the boy's head, prayed for him and then forgot all about it. At about the same time I heard through one of the guards that my life was at risk."

"You must have been terrified, Jon. You know they broadcast a death threat."

"Well, I think that death threat actually happened later, after they decided to let me go. They were just making noise, trying to draw attention to me one last time so someone would offer them money. I'm sure that's why they made the videotape, too.

"But listen to this—the little boy's skin cleared up within a week after I prayed for him. And when his father told the kidnappers about it, it terrified them! They were afraid of me, and even more afraid to kill me. Once the boy was healed, they wanted me out of there. They thought I had some sort of power they didn't understand."

"You did."

"Right. I did."

"You know I prayed that you'd get that letter and poem. In fact several people prayed with me. This old friend of mine from college wrote to me after she saw our story on the news. Her husband's an Episcopal priest."

"So she and her husband prayed for me?"

"She and her husband and their church, Jon. I've never met people quite like that."

"By the way, how are Jim Richards and Joyce doing?"

"They did everything they could to help you. I'll tell you all about Jim's hard work later. But what about this other story of yours? What about the spiritual release you mentioned?"

Jon yawned and rubbed his eyes. "Betty, I've been talking too long, and I'm tired. Can we just go for a walk or something and not talk for awhile?"

"Do you want me to go back to my room?"

"Are you kidding?" Jon gave her a sly look. "I'm not letting you out of my sight this time. If I rest, you rest too. Understood?"

Betty looked sheepishly at him. "Understood."

"Betty . . . ," He turned toward her and gently held her upper arms in his hands. "Are you sure there's nothing going on between you and this Mike person?" Again, sadness shadowed his face.

Betty shook her head in amazement. "Jon, you're being unreasonable." She tried to make her voice sound calm and reassuring. "Mike was a good friend during your captivity. In fact if it hadn't been for him, you'd never have received the letter and poem. But your captivity is over, and as far as I'm concerned, I don't care if I see him again. Mike's history."

"Are you sure?"

"Jon, I'm sure! Now let it go, okay?"

By now Jon was looking sheepish. "Okay, Betty. I love you, that's all."

"I love you too, Jon. I'm not interested in anyone else." She paused briefly. "Don't you believe me?" Her face was beginning to register annoyance, and Jon saw it.

He paused, narrowed his eyes and scrutinized her playfully. "Okay, okay. I believe you. Subject closed."

"My spiritual release started with a dream, Betty."

"What kind of a dream?"

Despite a nap and a walk, Jon was still unclear in his thinking. He struggled to find the right words, but never quite came up with them. His mind drifted from one subject to another, causing him to forget what he'd started to say in the first place. Frustrated and weary, he put his arm around Betty, pulling her close and resting his head on hers.

"I'm going to try and tell you what it was like there, in Beirut, in that hole. Maybe the story will make more sense if you can picture it for yourself."

Quietly and simply, Jon recreated his ordeal, so recent and vivid in his mind. And for the moment, as she closed her eyes and listened, Betty found herself imprisoned with him. It was dark, the smell in the air was foul, and Jon's mood was one of incomparable despair.

Jon had been held captive for nearly five months. Of the various men who guarded him, few spoke English. And only two of them actually conversed with him from time to time. Otherwise he had been painfully alone, bored and uncomfortable, visited only by unwelcome intruders such as guilt, fear, self-pity, and disbelief.

It seemed that just as he'd overcome one inner adversary, another would arise with its own set of allegations. Quiet as the fetid cellar was, there was no peace within him. Jon was tortured by his own thoughts, which troubled him nearly as much as his chain and blindfold. Even the Bible his captors had given him seemed more condemning than comforting.

As he slept restlessly one night, he dreamed of distorted images and incomprehensible scenarios. Just as he was waking, however, he clearly saw a book. On the cover was only one word written in red—TRUTH. Once he'd read the word, he awoke, immediately pondering the significance of the dream.

What did truth have to do with his plight? Puzzled and perplexed, he tried to shake off the impression that the dream was significant. But from time to time, he could see the book and its crimson title in his mind, demanding further consideration.

"Truth . . . ," he muttered under his breath. "What does truth have to do with anything?"

The inner reply came to him immediately. *You will know the truth, and the truth will set you free.*

Jon responded strangely to the thought. He found himself blinking back tears. "God knows I want to be free. But what does truth have to do with freedom?"

He determined that he would seek out every fragment of truth that could possibly pertain to his circumstances.

"I am a hostage. I am chained to a wall. I am blindfolded. I am helpless . . ."

No, you are not helpless. That isn't true.

Jon reconsidered. His mind was functioning, so he could think. His spirit was bruised, but still believed in

God, so he could pray. He had been given a Bible, so he could read it. His body was confined but still able to move, so he could choose to exercise.

Jon's process of mentally listing truths continued for hours. It became almost a game, often interrupted by the voice of reason.

"I am here because someone wants to use me for some purpose. I am here because I took a deadly chance in coming to Beirut. I am here because I deserve to be here . . ."

No, you do not deserve to be here. That isn't true.

"Okay, so God isn't punishing me. And I'm not going to die here. I'm not a born loser. And He hasn't forgotten me."

To his amazement, Jon found that his quest for truth seemed to be weakening the power of the unpleasant emotions that had haunted him for months. And gradually, almost imperceptibly, a new premise began to spring forth from his faith in a Sovereign God.

"I have to believe I'm here for a purpose. But what?"

Jon reflected on other times in his life when he'd felt helpless, entangled in various webs of circumstance that seemed unyielding in their power over him. Problems with his mother. Difficulties in school. His wretched marriage. Those had been far less traumatic confinements, but they had immobilized him, nevertheless.

And how had he escaped? In every case, once he had stopped denying the bleak reality of his situation, he had been able to identify the steps he needed to take. When he'd unflinchingly confronted his problems, he had always found a way out.

"The common denominator was truth. Once I faced the truth, I was set free. But this time there are no steps I can take."

That isn't true. God is going to set you free. So you can get ready to go home.

"I can't see any reason to believe that God is going to set me free."

Believe it by faith. Faith is the evidence of the unseen.

"It wasn't easy, Betty. From time to time I was back to my old pattern of blaming myself, fearing death, wallowing in self-pity, and thinking God had forgotten me."

Jon scrupulously avoided telling Betty about his mighty bout with guilt over his first marriage. He wasn't sure he wanted her to know how seriously he had doubted his qualifications for being a good husband.

"But, little by little, I found myself confronting each of those moods with the truth—that God was in charge, that I wasn't paying for past sins, and that He was going to set me free."

"So how did you prepare for your freedom?"

"By believing it was coming! By planning my conversations with you. By exercising and trying to stay in some sort of physical shape. And by refusing to give in to all the negative feelings."

Betty suddenly remembered the woman who had spoken at Erica's women's group. Ruth somebody. She had virtually said the same thing. "Jon, do you know what God's purpose was in letting you be kidnapped?"

"I'm really not sure, at least not yet. But maybe somehow I can help other people who are struggling with something. Do you know what I mean?"

Betty nodded. "Trapped is trapped," she said, remembering some of her own desperate moments.

"That's right," Jon smiled. "And truth is truth."

"Jim? It's me, Betty! How are you?"

Jim's voice was sharp with excitement. "Betty! Is Jon with you?"

"He's right here and he wants to talk to you. But listen, Jim. You've got to tell me what to do. The State

Department paid my way here from Nairobi, and they'll either pay my way back to Kenya or to California. But Jim, I never even got to Uganda. All that airfare has been wasted. Should I just go on to Africa and meet Jon in California later?"

Oh, God. Please make him say no.

"Betty, you can't leave Jon now."

"I don't want to leave him, Jim. And of course he doesn't want me to go. But what about the money? We're talking about more than two thousand dollars."

"You come back here with Jon, and we'll figure out some way to pay for it. There's no way you're going to Africa now, Betty. That would be ridiculous at this point. Maybe you can both go together in a few weeks."

"Are you sure?"

"Of course I'm sure. Now let me talk to Jon."

Betty listened with a smile as the two friends joked with each other about Jon's Beirut interlude. Jon's face almost glowed as he spoke.

With every passing day, he had become much more his old self. His mental focus had improved, his fear of crowds had diminished, and he was beginning to talk about the future with genuine interest. The only thing he couldn't seem to grasp was his international "fame." After the call to California, he and Betty briefly greeted the throng of reporters lining the fence. And as they walked around the hospital grounds, Jon grew thoughtful.

"You know, I've worked in the media for years, and I've seen these flash-in-the-pan stories happen to other people. I've even contributed to them. But this is my first time on the receiving end. You've been faced with this for months, haven't you? How have you handled it?"

Betty had to laugh. "Well at first it was rather fascinating. In fact I'd say the intrigue of being on the news sort of numbed me to the initial pain of your kidnapping.

And in the beginning I got a lot of supportive letters from complete strangers who were horrified by your disappearance and the canceled wedding. Most people really do have big hearts. But it doesn't take long to get tired of the intrusion."

"I'll tell you what I don't understand. Why are they treating me like a hero? I sat out six months of life in my underwear, and then all of a sudden I was released. Some guys have been in there for years, and it sounds like they're still sane and hopeful. They're the heroes."

"I guess it's the same thing you were talking about before. Lots of people are stuck in their own miserable circumstances, and for the moment, you symbolize freedom to them. You overcame adversity and survived. Maybe it gives people hope just to see that you made it."

Jon looked at Betty, still marveling at the miracle of her presence beside him. He abruptly changed the subject.

"When are we getting married, Betty? Shall we find a chaplain and get it over with here?"

"Get it over with? Is that how you feel about marrying me?"

He shook his head. "That's how I feel about waiting. What are we waiting for?"

Betty considered his question with ambivalence. She envisioned a romantic, candlelit wedding. She remembered her ice-blue silk dress, still encased in plastic. Then she thought about all the phone calls she would have to make, the invitations that would have to be written, all the arrangements another ceremony would require. Jon was right. It would be easier to get it over with. "There's just one thing that bothers me about getting married here, Jon."

Jon felt an unexpected rush of insecurity. "What's that?"

"The people that prayed for you, for us. There are so many new friends you've never even met. The guys that recorded my song. The men and women at Erica's church. Even some of the reporters in L.A. really seemed to care. A lot of those people made me promise that they'd be invited to the wedding. And I said yes."

"Well, if that's a way I can thank people for praying, then let's do it."

"I think that's what it's really all about. And there's another thing. Erica's husband Ken is an Episcopal priest. And I've been thinking that I'd like for him to perform the wedding ceremony. You'll like him a lot. And for some reason, I just know he'll have some wonderful things to say to us."

Jon brushed his hand across her hair. "Your life has changed a lot in the past six months, hasn't it, Betty? And I have a feeling the changes have been more good than bad.

Betty had yet to describe her own ordeal for him. The bitter tears. The crippling depression. The brutal disappointments. The near-breaking point.

All at once she remembered the inner promise she had received in answer to her most desperate prayer. "Jon is alive . . . he stills loves you . . . he will soon be free."

In Jon's ordeal, and in hers, there had been a common ground. They had both been powerless. God had met them in their despair. He had revealed truth to them.

And it was that truth, once they had chosen to believe it, that had set each of them free—first in spirit, then in actual fact.

10

$\mathcal{D}$ense fog had shrouded Laguna Beach all night. By eleven in the morning the sun was beginning to make its presence known, and by the time Betty and Jon arrived at Victoria Beach the sky had taken on a delicate blue opalescence. The sea was almost silent, lapping against damp rocks. Seabirds cried out across the still gray water as the couple made their way over stone and sand to the base of the old tower.

"It's cold," Betty shivered, untying a teal green sweater around her shoulders and pulling it over her head. "I thought it was supposed to be in the seventies today." She shoved her hands in her jeans pockets, trying to keep them warm.

"I'm going to see if my cameras still work," Jon said as he started to tinker with one of his Nikons. Vince Angelo had shipped Jon's equipment to Betty after the kidnapping, and he wasn't quite willing to believe that the sensitive controls had survived the journey.

She watched him as he tiptoed around tide pools, focusing and refocusing on the beach's picturesque vistas. Soon Jon was actually to become her husband—the wedding had been rescheduled for the Saturday after next. With growing hope, Betty was beginning to imagine that their unusual love story really might have a storybook conclusion after all.

Betty and Jon had returned from Weisbaden just over a month before. By now the media attention had died down, and although their wedding might have been fair game for the press, they had taken every precaution to ensure a meaningful and private ceremony at Ken and Erica's church. With that in mind, invitations had been re-sent, arrangements had been remade. More importantly, Jon had sworn on a Bible, on his grandparents' grave, and on all the stars in the heavens that he would not leave California before the wedding no matter what.

Betty noticed a folded piece of paper in her pocket. She reached in and pulled out a poem she had written. *Oh good. I almost forgot.* She'd intended to give it to Jon that day but had decided to read it one last time.

As diligently as she'd tried to write a joyful tribute to their love, the shadows of past fears and uncertainties still fell across her words.

Good grief. I hope he understands.

> Oh, come into my silence, Love,
> and teach me how to sing;
> lovely the song but I am afraid
> and courage is everything.
> Oh, come into my stillness, Love,
> and teach me how to dance;
> I feel the rhythm, I know the steps

and now I must take the chance.
Oh, come into my darkness, Love,
and teach me to believe;
Bright is the treasure, dazzling the gift
So how can I not receive?

She smiled to herself as she looked up at Jon squinting through his viewfinder. His love for her was a dazzling gift indeed. He was the only man she'd ever met who really cared about her, wholeheartedly loving the person she was on the inside. He'd helped her understand herself and had endowed her personality with a dimension of self-respect and confidence that had never been there before. Combined with her limitless admiration for Jon, their powerful spiritual bond, and a healthy physical attraction, they seemed to have everything they could possibly need to be happy together.

Any doubts she still held about the future had nothing to do with Jon's failures and weaknesses. She feared only her own shortcomings. The fact was, Betty's behavior in Germany with Mike Brody still troubled her. It reminded her of a long-ago incident during her first marriage. An old flame had erupted into a bit of an inferno one night during one of her husband's absences. Betty had barely escaped being consumed by the heat.

Was she a faithless lover by nature? The old question "Will love last?" had been answered months ago with the rather unsettling response: "It's up to you." Was Betty capable of making and keeping a marital commitment? No one on earth could be as perfectly suited to her as Jon Surrey-Dixon. She knew that to the depths of her soul. So why had she allowed someone else even to touch her?

When she glanced at Jon again, he was taking a photograph of her, the poem still in her hand. Before she could think to smile, the shutter clicked.

I'm glad he can't capture my thoughts on film.

Jon turned his back to the sun, removed a film cartridge from the camera and dropped it into his camera bag. When he sat down next to her on the cement step, she handed him the poem without a word.

He was silent for a few moments as he read it. Finally he said, "You're still afraid?"

She bit her lip. "Well, I'm really not. At least not as much as I was a few weeks ago. It's funny, because I wasn't really concerned at all when we were going to get married the first time. I was just starry-eyed and anxious to say you were mine once and for all."

"I guess we've both had a lot of time to think about marriage over the past seven months." His eyes narrowed as he appraised her sober face. "I hope you aren't changing your mind about getting married, Betty. Because I certainly haven't changed mine!"

She shook her head. "Of course I haven't. I would never change my mind."

He gently touched her face. "So what is it you're worried about?"

"Making sure our love lasts, Jon."

"Well if we made it through my captivity, surely we can make it through anything else. Is there something wrong, something I don't know about? I've noticed you've seemed a little, well, distant." He hesitated, weighing his words. "It's not something about that man you went out with in Germany . . . what's his name, Mike?"

"Oh, Jon," she groaned, wondering if he had been reading her mind a few moments before. "Please don't start that again! No, there's nothing wrong. I just don't want anything to *go* wrong. Everything is wonderful, and I guess I just don't want to ruin it somehow."

"Betty, I think our love is a gift from God. He's in it too, you know. Maybe it's more than a matter of believing in human love. Sometimes that isn't enough. Maybe it's about believing in Him too."

Teach me to believe.

Betty looked at her shoes for a full minute before she spoke. "Jon, there's something I haven't told you."

"What's that, Betty?"

"Something happened after you left, and I just think I should tell you."

"So tell me." His voice was gentle, but she could hear a subtle note of fear in it.

"About six weeks after you left I was feeling terrible— exhausted and lightheaded. I was in Washington D.C. at a hostage family get-together. In fact that's when I met Vince Angelo. My period was two weeks late. And Jon, I thought I was pregnant."

"So what happened?"

She shivered. There was no way he would ever comprehend the times of inner darkness she had passed through during his captivity. It was impossible to explain it now.

"I . . . I was feeling pretty despondent. You were gone, maybe forever. Here I'd been on television all over the world and was still being bombarded by reporters. And all I could think about was the shame of finding myself publicly pregnant and unmarried."

"Oh, Betty, I'm sorry. That was my fault . . ."

"No! No, it wasn't. If there was anyone to blame, it was me. I could have very easily said no, and I didn't want to."

He squeezed her hand. "I hate to say it, but I'm glad you didn't."

"I know. It was a fantastic night. But I want to tell you what happened. I actually called an abortion clinic and made an appointment. I hadn't even taken a test for pregnancy yet, so I wasn't sure whether I was or not. Of course they were very accommodating. They said I could be tested at the clinic and then just go ahead with the abortion if it came back positive."

"So did you go?"

"Well I struggled with the whole issue. The morality of abortion, the humiliation of pregnancy, the birth of a child without a father. I didn't know at that point if I'd ever see you alive again. I couldn't seem to come to any conclusion, so I got into a cab, and . . ."

"And did you go?"

She shook her head. "I couldn't, Jon."

"Why not? What finally made up your mind for you?"

"You, Jon! It was your baby too. I could have rationalized the rest, at least for the time being. But if a part of you was inside me, it was all I had left of you. How could I destroy your baby?"

Betty hadn't expected to cry. In fact she hadn't really meant to tell Jon all the grave details about the incident. She vividly remembered how she'd longed to be in his arms in Washington, feeling so desperately alone in that hotel room. Now, six months later, he was there, he knew, and he was holding her next to him, comforting her at last.

"I'm sorry, Betty." Jon took a deep breath before he spoke. His voice was husky with emotion. "Is that why you haven't wanted to make love to me since I got back?"

"That's one reason. The other reason is that I guess I just want to wait until we're married this time, so everything will be perfect. I think God might like it better that way, if you know what I mean. But, Jon, I want you more than ever."

He seemed bewildered. "Why didn't you talk to me about all this before? You just kept kind of pushing me away."

"I know. I'm sorry." Betty was as confused as he was. She shook her head, trying to explain her own actions.

"I guess I didn't want to discuss it with you outright because in spite of everything, I somehow wanted to keep that door open. I can't tell you how double-minded I've been, Jon. But after all we've gone through, I do want everything to be right."

He held her face against his, and brushed the back of her hair with his hand. "I want it to be right too. That's why I haven't made an issue of it. As long as there isn't anything else wrong . . ."

"There's nothing wrong, Jon. *Nothing*. I love you more than ever."

He sighed with evident relief. "Well, look, another week or so, and . . ." He kissed her sweetly. "I'm so glad we got that out in the open. I have to admit I've been feeling pretty bad."

"Forgive me, Jon. Really. I should have brought it up right away." Betty smiled at him gratefully, wiping her tears away with her hand.

He always understands. Always. It's amazing.

"So you like my new poem?"

"I love the poem, Betty. I love all your poems, but this one tells me our marriage is going to be all right." He looked at it again.

"Why does it tell you that?"

"Because it says that you're taking a step of faith. You're admitting you're afraid, but you're willing to sing, willing to dance, and you want to believe. I think God will take care of the rest."

Jon folded the paper and put in his shirt pocket. The sun was beginning to break through the pearly overcast as they left the tower behind. He took Betty's hand and began to laugh.

"Aren't we a pair? We love each other dearly, and we're both scared to death that getting married will ruin everything. Something tells me it's not supposed to be like that. Something tells me that we've got a lot to learn about marriage—*real* marriage."

The elegant entrance to the Ritz-Carlton Hotel framed two attractive couples as they greeted each other warmly. Jon and Betty, after a day at Laguna Beach, had managed to change clothes and were now properly attired for a stylish dinner with Erica and Ken Townsend at the five-star hotel just a few miles south of Victoria Beach.

"This is going to cost a fortune," Erica giggled as they strolled past the exquisite floral arrangements and fine art pieces that graced the hotel's lobby. "Are you sure you don't want to go to the Jolly Roger?"

"Don't be silly, Erica. No coffee shops tonight! Jon and I owe you two a lot more than a dinner at the Ritz."

Since their return to California, Ken had been preparing Jon and Betty for their wedding with a premarital counseling course he required all candidates for marriage to take. At first they had been a little put off by his insistence on the program—it seemed so unromantic and dull. But as each session came and went, they had found themselves addressing issues and concerns that could potentially damage their relationship.

On their way into Ken's office the week before, Betty had confided in Jon, "I guess all this is forcing us to be practical, even though I'd rather just go off somewhere and neck."

"Hold that thought," Jon had responded quite enthusiastically. "Who says we can't do both?"

In fact, their conversation at Victoria Beach earlier had sprung from Ken's demand that they be open and honest with each other, not hiding their innermost fears or frustrations. Ken was determined to provide the men and women he united in marriage with guidelines for living together. It was his wedding gift to them.

"Your name?" the tuxedoed host inquired.

"Surrey-Dixon. We have reservations for four."

"Right. This way, please."

They could hear rich arpeggios being played on a grand piano as they made their way through the well-appointed café. It was the least expensive dining room in the hotel, but still lavish enough to make them feel quite regal. Betty recognized the pianist's melody as the love theme from *Phantom of the Opera*. "Just love me, that's all I ask of you," the lyric said. It was one of her favorite songs.

Once they were settled at their table, a server brought their chosen bottle of wine and Ken proposed a toast. "Here's to a lifetime marriage and many, many years of love and understanding."

Glasses clinked. Betty caught Jon's eye and smiled at him. She said, "Ken, thank you for all you're doing to make that toast come true."

"Well, thank you for putting up with all my rhetoric," he laughed. "Poor Erica has to live with me, and she knows I don't always practice what I preach."

"You do pretty well, Ken," his wife patted his arm consol-ingly, "you really do."

"So what's the best marital advice you can give, Erica?" Jon asked the cleric's pretty wife.

She and Ken looked at each other for a moment before she answered. "Well, I'm sure you've already heard this from Ken, but we believe God is the third party in our marriage. The Bible says that a threefold cord is not easily broken, and our church considers marriage as one of the sacraments. That means that the Holy Spirit is invited into the union, and so His power becomes a factor in the relationship."

"That means it's not just a relationship between two people anymore." Ken completed his wife's thought. "It's sort of a holy love triangle."

She nodded. "It's a three-party agreement, and He's the one with the real power to keep it together."

"There's something else too." Ken added. "When you marry in the presence of other believers, you are asking them to agree with you in prayer. There's power in that too."

Jon said, "You know, Betty and I really thought about foregoing a formal ceremony and getting married by a chaplain in Weisbaden, but she wanted to invite a lot of friends to join us. I never thought about them agreeing with us in prayer, but it's a terrific idea, isn't it?"

"Jon, some couples think it's enough just to make love, to promise to be faithful to each other, and then to ask God's blessing on their agreement. But it's not enough at all. The church has been given authority by God to unite people in marriage. When a couple is married in the church, they aren't just promising to love forever. They are making a solemn vow to God and each other, and they're also receiving the Church's blessing."

Jon glanced at Betty. She lowered her eyes. They had experienced a remarkable sense of closeness after making love for the first time seven months before. They had quite seriously made a verbal marital commitment at that time. Yet they had both sensed that their personal covenant hadn't been complete.

"So you think that the church's blessing and the prayers of other Christians make for a stronger relationship?"

"Jon, the dynamic of prayer and the power of the Holy Spirit aren't just religious ideas. They are profound, dramatic realities."

Betty touched Erica's hand. Her question reflected the utmost concern of her heart. "So Erica, in light of that, you really believe love can last, don't you?"

Erica weighed her words carefully before she answered. "Well, that depends on what you mean by love, Betty. If you mean warm, fuzzy feelings, I'd have to say that they come and go. And if you mean passion, I'd say you have to work together at keeping that alive. But if you are asking if a loving relationship can last, of course it can. It not only lasts, it grows stronger and deeper with every passing year."

Ken nodded, reading Betty's need for further reassurance. "Betty, this is your second marriage, and it's mine too. If you're like me, you've blamed yourself for a lot of things that went wrong the first time. Some of it may have been your fault, and it's good if you can acknowledge that. But it takes two people to make a marriage work. And they not only have to agree to make it work, they have to be *capable* of making it work."

"That's why it's important to make the right choice in the first place," Erica commented. "You can't just bring God into the picture and expect Him to change somebody's entire personality."

Jon sighed. "That's interesting. You know, when I was in Beirut, I struggled with that very issue. I found myself taking all the blame for my first marriage's collapse. I felt like such a failure, I even wondered if it was wrong for me to marry Betty. But you're right—it takes two people.

"When I'm realistic about it, Carla simply wasn't emotionally capable of being married—at least not to me.

Even though she would pretend to repent and reform, she had no real intention of changing. I certainly didn't do everything perfectly either, but I did my best. Looking back now, I really think I did."

"I wish I could say that myself," Ken scrutinized his wine glass as he spoke. "I didn't really do very much right at all. I came into my marriage to Erica knowing I had blown it the first time, and I mean I *really* blew it. But even at that, God has met me in my weaknesses and given me His strength. No matter how badly things have gone wrong in the past, it's all forgiven and forgotten. And the future belongs to Him."

Their conversation was interrupted by the arrival of four artfully designed salads, and they all fell into admiring silence as they were being served. Betty felt warm and hopeful, encouraged by the exchange of ideas.

Thank God I insisted we wait to get married. I'm so glad Ken could be part of this.

"Ken, why don't you ask the blessing on this food," Jon suggested. They all joined hands as Ken began to pray,

> Our Father, we thank you for Jon and Betty, for their lives and the tremendous plans you have for them.
>
> We ask that their feelings of love for each other be sustained.
>
> We ask that the high esteem they have for each other remain untarnished.
>
> We ask that Your wise counsel and strengthening presence never be ignored.
>
> And we ask that the privilege of prayer always

be exercised in their home, as they invite You to be
the third party in their marriage.

Thank you for this happy occasion, for the food,
and for the blessing of friendship.

For Jesus' sake, Amen.

Betty was trying to remember every word of Ken's
prayer. *I wish I had that in writing. I'd sign it.*

Erica's curiosity brought a lighter tone to the conversation. "So Betty, tell me about your honeymoon plans,
or is that top secret information?"

"Only to a point. We're certainly not giving out
addresses or phone numbers. But I can tell you this
much—we were going to London for our honeymoon
the last time, and we were planning to stay through
Christmas. This time it looks like the best we can do is
celebrate the Queen's birthday there, but that's what
we're going to have to do."

"Are you going to be in a hotel?"

"Oh, no way. That would cost a fortune. A friend of
Jon's has offered us a flat outside the city, about twenty
minutes from town by train, and he's also leaving us his
car. We can use his place for a month's time, and after
that we're going on to Africa to finish the report I was
supposed to be doing when Jon was released."

"That all sounds splendid. Can we come too? I could
use a nice vacation about now." Ken winked at Erica.

"Sorry," Jon held up both hands. "This dinner is all
you're getting out of our deal—no tagging along on our
honeymoon, thank you very much, no matter how helpful you've been. I just hope some creative genius reporter
doesn't try to follow us around England hoping for a
tabloid scoop: 'Former Hostage On Secret Honeymoon
in London!'"

Once dinner was finished, they toured the hotel together—gift shops, pools, gardens, and verandas, finally saying their farewells while they waited for their cars. "We've got one more session with you, Ken. We'll see you Wednesday afternoon."

"Thanks so much for a delightful evening," Ken waved good-bye as he tipped the valet and got into the driver's seat.

Erica hugged her friend warmly. She looked into Betty's eyes and quietly said, "Don't worry so much Betty. There really are happy endings in life, and you're going to have one. I believe it with all my heart. You'll see!"

> Let me not to the marriage of true minds
> Admit impediments; love is not love . . .
> Which alters when it alteration finds . . .

Jon Surrey-Dixon quoted the sonnet with surprising aplomb, holding his bride's hands in his.

> . . . Or bends with the remover to remove.
> O, No, it is an ever-fixed mark
> That looks on tempests and is never shaken;
> It is the star to every wand'ring bark,
> Whose worth's unknown, although his height be taken.

Betty, speaking as courageously as possible, continued the recitation,

> Love's not Time's fool, though rosy lips and cheeks
> Within his bending sickle's compass come;
> Love alters not with his brief hours and weeks,
> But bears it out even to the edge of doom.

If this be error, and upon me proved,
I never writ, nor no man ever loved.

The soft music of guitar and flute continued to play after the sonnet had been completed. The church was fragrant with flowers and bathed in candlelight. Father Kenneth Townsend stood solemnly facing the congregation, resplendent in his finest robes.

"Dearly beloved," he read, "we have come together in the presence of God to witness and bless the joining together of this man and this woman in Holy Matrimony . . .

"The union of husband and wife in heart, body, and mind is intended by God for their mutual joy; for the help and comfort given one another in prosperity and adversity; and, when it is God's will, for the procreation of children and their nurture in the knowledge and love of the Lord. Therefore marriage is not to be entered into unadvisedly or lightly, but reverently, deliberately and in accordance with the purposes for which it was instituted by God . . ."

The pews were filled with well-wishers. Old friends and new ones were seated next to each other, watching the proceedings with extraordinary interest. Vince Angelo had flown in from New York. David Jacobsen, the former hostage, sat with his son Eric. Several Los Angeles news reporters and television personalities were present. Even Red Jeffrey, Harold Fuller's cranky Marine Corps friend, was there in full-dress uniform.

The bride wore a gown of shimmering ice-blue silk, with strands of pearls braided into her hair. She carried long-stemmed white roses tied with a blue satin ribbon. There was no fear on her face, and although she wasn't quite smiling, hope surged in her heart and shined out through her eyes.

At her left was her matron-of-honor, aglow with joy, seated in her ubiquitous wheelchair. No one but Joyce Jiminez could have been at Betty's side on that particular occasion. The two women had little in common but their mutual faith, their dedication to Christian humanitarianism, and their common concern for Jon Surrey-Dixon. But that was reason enough to provide the diminutive Hispanic woman with an honored role at the wedding.

The groom was dressed in a traditional tuxedo, a white rose in his lapel. At his right stood Jim Richards, his old friend, and a fiercely loyal one at that. If no one else had been there to pray, the handful of people who stood at the front of the church would have stormed the gates of heaven themselves, pleading for a blessed future for the bride and groom.

As the ceremony progressed, an unusual group of men gathered at the left of the altar. They were dressed somewhat more carefully than usual, but Brian Demetrius' band still had a uniquely ragged look. When they began to sing, however, their hair styles, earrings, and attire were quickly forgotten. Betty's song would never sound more beautiful.

> . . . Lands and oceans come between us,
> People, places, months and years,
> But the eyes of God have seen us,
> And He's smiled through His tears.
> He knows the way, He has the answer,
> Somehow, some day we'll never say good-bye . . .

At last, that some day had come. Jon drew an unsteady breath as the song finished. Memories of his nightmare in Lebanon had caught him off guard. The miracle of the song, of hearing it for the first time in answer to an urgent prayer brought a flood of tears to his eyes. He shook his head and smiled at Betty, who was trying to retain her own composure. Not surprisingly, the guests at the wedding were also moved by the lyrics, and by the popular band's willingness to perform it in such a private, sacred setting.

Father Ken turned toward the bride.

"Elisabeth Fuller Casey, will you have this man to be your husband, to live together in the covenant of marriage? Will you love him, comfort him, honor and keep him in sickness and in health, and, forsaking all others, be faithful to him as long as you both shall live?"

God, you know I mean it. Don't let me fail again.

"I will," she responded, firmly and with all the determination she could muster.

"Jonathan Keith Surrey-Dixon, will you have this woman to be your wife, to live together in the covenant of marriage? Will you love her, comfort her, honor and keep her, in sickness and in health, and, forsaking all others, be faithful to her as long as you both shall live?"

"I will," Jon replied, looking into Betty's eyes, hoping his voice wouldn't break.

"Who gives this woman to be married to this man?"

Harold P. Fuller stood ramrod straight in his best suit, starched white shirt, and black necktie. "I do!" he barked just a little too loudly. Relieved to have his responsibilities behind him, he sank into his assigned pew, praying from the depths of his soul that this would be his daughter's last wedding.

Betty handed her roses to Joyce, and she and Jon stood hand in hand, repeating their vows. The words sounded like poetry ". . . for better, for worse, for richer for poorer, in sickness and in health, to love and to cherish . . ." Had she ever really made those promises before? No, never like this.

Once their rings had been exchanged, Father Ken joined Jon and Betty's right hands together and pronounced them man and wife. "Those whom God has joined together let no one put asunder."

The congregation was led in prayers for Jon and Betty's future life together. As Betty listened, she longed for them to be literally fulfilled. Were people really paying attention to the words?

". . . that each may be to the other a strength in need, a counselor in perplexity, a comfort in sorrow and a companion in joy."

"Amen."

". . . Give them grace, when they hurt each other, to recognize and acknowledge their fault, and to seek each other's forgiveness and yours."

"Amen."

"Make their life together a sign of Christ's love to this sinful and broken world, that unity may overcome estrangement, forgiveness heal guilt, and joy conquer despair."

"Amen."

"Give them such fulfillment of their mutual affection, that they may reach out in love and concern for others."

"Amen."

Betty and Jon had elected to have a communion service during the wedding. Once it was completed, and the benediction spoken, the musicians began to play Bach's beloved melody, "Jesu, Joy of Man's Desiring." The bride and groom turned, smiled radiantly at their friends and swept down the center aisle together. As they reached the back of the church, Jon glanced at Betty who was still fighting tears. "It's too late for you to change your mind now, Mrs. Surrey-Dixon."

"Not a chance," she laughed, kissing his cheek. "I'm

not going anywhere. Besides, you're the one who ran away the last time."

He took her in his arms and held her. He was just about to kiss her with his whole heart and soul and mind. Suddenly the church's rather elderly wedding coordinator impatiently interrupted their embrace and herded them into the social hall at a brisk pace.

"You stand here," the bespectacled woman commanded. "No, not *there*. You stand *here!*"

She took Betty by the arm and led her to an invisible spot. "And the bride stands *here*."

Betty scowled rebelliously. *And you stand right over there, little lady, right outside the door.*

Jon, who was feeling benevolent at the moment, squeezed his wife's arm. He gave her a kind but cautionary look.

Jon and Betty were soon joined by Jim, Joyce, Harold, Ken, and Erica. Fortunately, as if by magic, the cranky wedding coordinator utterly vanished.

Before long the air was bright with flashbulbs. The sound of laughter filled the room. Along with their guests, the bride and groom celebrated their long-awaited wedding by cutting a tiered cake, posing for photographs, and opening gifts. Friends and loved ones had brought their own particular best wishes and presents and dozens more had come by mail.

There were greetings from David and Peggy Say. "I told you he'd be out soon!" Peggy's note reminded Betty. A $25 check had come from Ricky Simms Ministries with a letter inviting the happy couple to participate in a "Free-at-Last Interview." Arthur Nichols, who had denied milk to starving babies not many months before, sent a card and a personal check for $500.

There was nary a word from Mike Brody. After debating with herself for days about risks versus the rudeness involved in inviting or not inviting him, she'd finally done so, pretending she hadn't seen herself address the envelope and praying that he'd ignore it. She'd actually been half afraid he'd show up at the wedding.

To her immense relief, he hadn't.

In the midst of all this, the bride and groom raised their glasses with their friends in a series of heartfelt toasts to all their tomorrows.

"Here's to a wonderful honeymoon!"

"Here's to a healthy, wealthy future!"

"Here's to good friends and happy memories!"

"Here's to no more trips to Beirut!"

Mrs. Kenneth Townsend leaned across her husband and spoke discreetly to Mrs. Jon Surrey-Dixon. "Here's to that love story with a happy ending," she whispered with a broad grin.

Betty smiled hopefully at Erica, nodding her head in full agreement. She had just given Jon a wedding surprise—two round-trip tickets to Hawaii to be used within the year, secretly financed by Harold P. Fuller. "You'd better get this one off to a good start," he'd gruffly warned his daughter.

But the most unexpected gift came back to Betty from her own heart, from her own pen. Just as the reception was ending, Jon presented the new Mrs. Surrey-Dixon with a wedding gift only he could have created. It was a sepia-tone photograph of her, taken just a week and a half before as she sat at the foot of the Victoria Beach tower. She was gazing pensively toward the camera, her hair windblown, a poem in her hand.

Along the side of the tower, was printed a verse she had

written and all but forgotten. It had been among the first group of poems she'd sent to Jon, before they'd ever met.

"This is my prayer—our prayer—for our marriage, for our home, for our new life together," Jon remarked softly. Everyone fell silent as he read the simple rhyme aloud.

> For our fears, give us courage.
> In our tears, find a song,
> For our doubts, grant conviction,
> Where we're weak, make us strong.
> Turn our faults into blessings,
> Turn our griefs into praise,
> And for dark hours of sadness
> Give us bright, golden days.